Just The Beginning

Just The Beginning

By Betty Miles

AN AVON CAMELOT BOOK

AVON BOOKS
A division of
The Hearst Corporation
1790 Broadway
New York, New York 10019

First Camelot Printing, April, 1978

CAMELOT TRADEMARK REG. U.S. PAT. OFF. AND IN
OTHER COUNTRIES, MARCA REGISTRADA, HECHO EN
U.S.A.

Printed in the U.S.A.

BAN 20 19 18 17 16 15 14 13

Just The Beginning

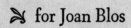 for Joan Blos

One

I think this is the worst day of my whole life.

I am thirteen. Three hundred and sixty-five days a year for thirteen years makes almost five thousand days. And this one is the worst of all.

Worse than the day when I stole a dollar from my mother's dresser and bought a Princess Pat Paper Doll set. Worse than the Christmas Day when my sister Julia's appendix burst and we had to wait two hours at the hospital to find out if she'd be all right. Even worse than the day last year when I had to bring home my report card with a *D* in social studies. ("Oh, Catherine!" my mother said. "A *D*!")

Two awful things are going to happen today. The first one is that my mother is going to be a cleaning lady.

In Camden Woods, where we live, lots of people *have* cleaning ladies. I see them when I visit friends. At Amy's house the cleaning lady comes to the back door in her regular clothes with her cleaning-lady dress in a shopping bag. She changes in the bathroom. At lunch time, Amy's mother sets places in the dining room for us and Amy's little sisters, but the cleaning lady eats by herself in the kitchen. Amy's sisters always make a mess in the playroom—they spill pieces of games all over the floor and build houses with the couch cushions and throw their candy papers around—and the cleaning lady is supposed to clean it all up. I always feel funny at Amy's house on cleaning lady days.

Our town is one of the ten richest towns in the whole United States. But not everybody who lives here is rich. We're not. My father just owns a candy and newspaper store called Bob's. My mother has always stayed at home. But she's not the kind of housewife who sits around and watches TV with curlers in her hair. Mom works hard. She makes slipcovers for the furniture and curtains for all the windows. She raises vegetables in the back yard and she cans and freezes what we don't eat. She does all the ordering for Dad's store. She can put up bathroom tile and mend rugs. Mom's so good at doing things.

But when she decided to look for steady work, it seemed as though the things she can do didn't count. She advertised for sewing to do at home, but it was too irregular and she didn't charge enough to make it worthwhile. She answered ads in the paper for women to work part-time, but they wanted you to sell thousands of awful greeting cards or to call people up and say they had won some "free prize" and get them to buy light bulbs or pencils. Finally Mom went to the State Employment Agency. They told her how tight things were: only part-time jobs for salesladies and cashiers, nothing at all in bookkeeping, and people wanted younger women for receptionists. When Mom came back from her appointment she said she had made up her mind. She was going to do house cleaning.

When Aunt Rose heard about it she said, "Please, Clara, don't be so quick to demean yourself."

She really meant, "to demean *us*." I know she did. Aunt Rose always worries about what other people say. I hate to think I could take after her. "That kind of work isn't for someone like you," she said. "Let those people sitting around on welfare get out and do it. What you want is a job in some nice office."

But the way Mom explained it, she didn't have much choice. "I don't have the right training for a secretarial job," she said. "They want shorthand and seventy-words-a-minute typing or else they want young girls they can train fast. Not somebody my age."

"Seems to me they'd be better off with a reliable, mature woman," Dad said.

"Well, that's not what the Employment Agency people told me," Mom answered. "They said I ought to go out for factory work. But it would just kill me to sit still all day doing the same thing over and over. It seems a shame there's no money to hire school aides. That's what I'd like to do, if I had my choice. But they say there's always a big demand for houseworkers. And housework pays the same as factory work—not that it's much, just the bare minimum wage. But I'd have a change of scene every day and see the inside of some houses I always wished I could walk around in. Anyway, no one can say I'm not an experienced housecleaner!"

That was last week. I didn't expect Mom to start work so soon. But she's been worrying about money, and once she makes up her mind to do something, she wants to get out and do it. I just can't get used to the idea of Mom starting to be a cleaning lady. This day of all days.

Dad hugged Mom before he left to open the store. He doesn't usually do that, but I know he loves my mother. They have been married for twenty years. Dad is partly bald, with fuzzy hair around his bare spot. Sometimes I wish he was handsome and young and had to run for the 8:05 train with a briefcase like other people's fathers, but most of the time I'm glad he's the way he is. You could go up to Dad on the street if you were lost and ask for help—he's that kind of person. What he cares about most is his family—Mom and Julia and me. I know he's worried about Mom doing housework. Soon he's going to be worried about me.

Mom watched Dad back our old car down the driveway. Then she let the curtain drop and began to clear the table.

"Don't, Mom," Julia said. "We'll do it."

I was about to run upstairs for a scarf when I heard Julia say "we." I came back and began to put the butter and jam away as though it was my idea too, but that wasn't the same as doing it naturally, like Julia. I really want to do kind and helpful things, but sometimes I just get involved with my own problems and forget. Right then I was worrying so much about how I was going to hurt Mom that I didn't even think about being helpful in an ordinary way. That's me!

Mom stood in the doorway as though she didn't want to leave. Mom is heavier than some mothers, but she has a comfortable look that those thin ones don't have. She doesn't wear clanky bracelets or silk shirts or blue jeans like lots of women in Camden Heights. Mom wears dresses. I think Mom is beautiful. She has thick black hair and a sudden smile. But she wasn't smiling this morning.

"Dad minds too much," she said. "I worry about it."

"Don't worry, Mom," Julia said.

I wished that I could tell her that. But I was going to worry her more.

"Will you keep on at Allen School, Mom?" I asked. She is a volunteer helper in the first grade at Allen, where Julia and I went.

"I don't know, honey. I'll just have to take one day at a time and see how things work out. I'm afraid I'll probably have to stop."

"I bet they'll be sorry if you leave. I bet you're the best reading volunteer they've ever had."

"Oh, Catherine," Mom said. "What I do isn't all that important. Anyone who just sits down and listens to a child in that noisy classroom is helpful. They'll find somebody else. But I do hate to leave Bobby Arvin. He's just beginning to catch on that the words you read are the same as words you say. Last week I wrote

'Bobby eats spaghetti' on a piece of paper for him. He was so pleased, he carried that paper around and read it to everybody. He called it 'My Story.'"

"How could he read a word like 'spaghetti'?" I asked.

"Kids can read 'dinosaur' or 'Massachusetts' if they want to badly enough and you encourage them," Mom said. "But a quiet child like Bobby is liable to get lost in the shuffle without some extra attention."

Julia said, "It's late, Cath. We'd better go." She kissed Mom. "I hope you have a good day"

"Thank you, Julia," Mom said.

I didn't know what to say. What could I say?

"I wish you good luck in your work," I told her.

Mom smiled suddenly. "Thank you, Catherine. Have a good day now, both of you," she said.

A good day!

The really bad part of my day, the part no one but me knew about, was getting closer. All weekend I had meant to tell Julia, but somehow I never did. It's very hard to tell people your problems, even when you love them. I wish I could do it easier. I knew Julia could make me feel better, but I never seemed to find the right time to tell her. Now my whole family was going to find out.

The bus hadn't come, so we walked slowly.

"I wish Mom could do work she'd really like, like teaching," Julia said.

"I wish she'd do anything—even work in a factory!" I said. "Anything but housecleaning."

And I wish Dad didn't feel so bad about it. I know he would like to be able to support us himself. He says he was brought up that way, to think he should. The way Aunt Rose says: "The man is provider, the woman runs the house." But even though Dad works about ten hours a day at the store, he still doesn't earn very much. Julia's going to college next year and even if she gets a scholarship—I just know she will—she'll need extra money. Dad worries about that. The money Mom makes will help. I think Dad wouldn't mind Mom working if it was work she really liked. But he doesn't want her to have to clean other people's houses. I don't either. I wish I could get rid of this awful feeling that there's something shameful about it. Sometimes I just wish we were rich.

I asked Julia, "Did you ever wish we lived in a big house in The Woods and never had to worry about money?"

Julia laughed. "Of course. You know what I'd do the very first thing? Go to a shoe store and buy the exact pair of boots I wanted without even looking at the price tag."

"I'd buy a camel's-hair wrap coat," I said. "And a horse."

We both laughed. The bus rumbled onto Oak Street.

What I really wished for was not to have to go to school and hear the terrible news.

I was going to be suspended.

Two

The bus pulled up with its brakes screeching and kids yelling out the windows. Julia and I got on and the door slapped shut behind us. Julia went back to save a seat for Nathan and I sat down in the middle of the bus by a window. Once Mom saw us sitting like that. She couldn't believe it. "But you're sisters!" she said. "Don't you want to sit together?" That's the kind of thing you can't explain to a mother.

Our bus ride usually takes twenty minutes. I hoped it would be slow this morning because I needed time to think. You might wonder how a person *could* think, wedged into a seat with sixth-grade boys fighting and yelling around you, the bus engine shifting and grinding, and the driver's radio blaring out the "Hank Cummings Commuter Show." I can. I scrunch down into my coat, look out the window, tune out the noise, and think. It's a skill I've practiced since I started riding the bus two years ago, in sixth grade.

8

I have to be good at it, because George Waldman gets on two stops after me. George Waldman is a boy who has followed me around since kindergarten, throwing snowballs at me and stealing my lunch and tripping me up with his foot and laughing. He used to be a little boy in an earflap hat who chased me across the Allen School playground yelling, "I see Cathy's underpants!" I don't know why he chose me to pick on— maybe he knew I would be too scared to tell on him. The trouble is that George Waldman still picks on me and it is a lot worse now. George sits down right behind me every morning and he says in this low voice I'm supposed to overhear: "Wanna sell some dope?" or "Those hippie chicks are the best, oh yes."

George Waldman scares me. So I have learned to look out the window and think my own thoughts and ignore him as much as I can.

This morning I watched the town pass by and thought about suspension. I don't know how the school will tell my parents, or what they'll make me do for punishment. I know Aunt Rose will find out. She can always find something wrong with what we do: "Tell me, Clara, why you can't get Catherine to stand up straight—just look how she stoops!" or "I can't see any reason for Bob keeping such long hours when he hardly has any customers most of the time." Just wait till she hears about my suspension. Oh, boy.

Our bus route is like a guided tour of Camden Woods, going from ordinary blocks like ours to the curving roads with big houses in The Heights, all the way to The Woods where the estates are. After George

Waldman's stop we turn onto Broadway, which is the main street. We pass the dime store and the hardware store and a pizza parlor. Dad's store is next. Besides newspapers, Dad sells greeting cards and stationery supplies. He has a lunch counter, and there is always someone sitting there drinking coffee and looking at the paper and talking about the weather or hard times with Dad.

Dad's business is slow because most people get their newspapers delivered at home, and they don't go to Broadway so much since the new shopping mall opened. The mall has department stores and shoe stores and a fancy deli and the kind of stationery store that sells games and desk lamps and sunglasses and candles shaped like tree trunks and calendars with pictures of natural wonders or people in love or cats with clothes on. It's a much bigger store than Dad's.

Camden Heights is next. Amy, who's getting suspended with me, lives here, and so does Chris, but they go to school on a different bus. In Camden Heights there are big old houses with huge yards and big new development houses with small yards and swimming pools. Most people who live here work in the city. Amy's father does and so does Chris's. His mother works at home. She makes jewelry from gold and silver and real precious stones. I watch her sometimes when I visit Chris.

I don't call Chris my boyfriend—he's just a boy who is my friend. I don't want to have a boyfriend yet. I had one in fifth grade—Robert Blakely. He used to give me these smudgy, folded-up notes that said, "Dear

Catherine, I want to Kiss you." Robert Blakely was enough boyfriend for some time.

"C'mon, baby, you look so fine," George Waldman sang at me under his breath. He shifted his knees around so I could feel them through the back of the seat. "Oh, oh, yeah!" he sang. What a dope. I sat as still as I could with his knees poking me.

George said, "What's the matter, Cathy, you got bad troubles?" He drawled out the word "bad."

How could he know? It makes me furious to be so worried about my suspension when somebody like George Waldman gets suspended hundreds of times and probably doesn't even mind. George and his friends are one of the gangs in our school. They hang around in a pack outside, lighting up cigarettes, punching each other, picking on people. Like Karen. If she goes anywhere near those guys they say, "Hey Skinny, how's the weather up there?" or worse. They whistle and laugh and make disgusting remarks. Sometimes they start fights. Once one of them punched Chris in the stomach for no reason. Chris nearly fell over. This kid just walked away laughing. I don't think our school cares much whether people like George stay around or drop out.

There are a lot of different groups in our school. School-spirit kids who join all the clubs and wear school jackets and go out for football or cheerleading. People who make all A's and join the honor society and get involved in student government. The kids other kids call hippies, who wear patched-up jeans and expensive hiking boots. I am friends with a lot of different kids. Most of them do well in school. I'm more sort of average. One problem I have is that I never feel exactly sure where I fit in.

Julia's always been sure of herself. She is one of the best students in Camden High, which is right next to our school with a row of trees between. So is Nathan. He's a photographer, and he's taking most of the pictures for the yearbook, which Julia's editor of. They work late after school, when Julia isn't checking at the A&P and sometimes they work at our house at night. Nathan might take my picture for the candid section of the yearbook, even though I'm just in junior high. I hope so. I hate to come right out and ask him, though.

I think Nathan and Julia are a perfect match. I wish they would keep on with their romance and get married and have a child so that I could be an aunt. But Julia says she won't even think about getting married for years.

Julia's going to be a city planner. She has applied to Yale and M.I.T. and Barnard, and also to Camden Community College in case the others don't accept her. I know they will. Julia is just plain brilliant. She is going to be the valedictorian of her class. She made all A's in junior high and high school. She took every class in mechanical drawing the school gives, and they had to make up an advanced one just for her.

I sometimes wish I was like Julia, so smart and sure of what I wanted to be. I always wonder how people decide. Do people who sell shoes really want to? How does it work out that some people drive buses and some are lawyers and other people work in factories? Guidance counselors say you should go to college to learn how to be what you want to be. But what if you don't even know what you want to be? Where do you find out?

Besides, lots of people never go to college at all. Look at Mom. She stayed home after high school to take care of her little sisters because her mother was sick. Then she married Dad and they moved to Camden Woods. She helped with the store at first, but she couldn't keep on working there when Julia and I were little. It doesn't seem fair that she's worked so hard all her life and never got any money for it. I wonder how Mom's day will be. I wonder if she'll eat in the kitchen. I would hate it if she has to clean up some girl's room like mine. That would be disgusting. I think people should do their own cleaning or else live in their own mess.

"Wake up, Cathy," George whispered. "Time for school."

Not quite. We just turned into The Woods. Karen lives here. Karen's getting suspended with me. Karen's father is a banker who actually knows the President. Her mother is the editor of a woman's magazine—not *Ms.*, but the housekeeping kind. Karen has her own bathroom and her own TV and her own horse. She might seem like a strange friend for me to have, but she's not. We like the same books and the same jokes, and we have other friends between us, like Amy. Now we have the same worry about getting suspended.

Karen's parents want her to go to boarding school next year. They say she needs a good start to get into the right college. I wonder if I would get into the right college if I went to boarding school. I wonder what the right college is.

George Waldman pulled my hair. "End of the line," he said, sort of spitting in my ear. He can make the most ordinary words sound like a horrible message. The sixth-grade boys yelled louder, as usual, when the bus turned into the school driveway. Then they all stood up and started pushing toward the door.

"Hold it, hold it," the bus driver said, as he says every morning. "Sit down till we stop."

The boys pushed back into their seats, falling on top of each other and yelling.

I always wait till last, so I can walk off the bus calmly. Sometimes George Waldman waits even longer and follows me, but this time he jumped out of his seat as soon as the bus stopped. He was carrying a notebook and a pencil and a brown paper bag, and he hit people on the head with the notebook as he went past.

The bus was late—we were just in time for the bell. Pushing time. We heaved toward the gym door.

"Hey, look out! That's my foot."

"Move over, Fatso."

"C'mon—push!"

Finally we were inside. I went to my locker, got my books, and looked around for Karen and Amy. I didn't see them, so I headed toward the principal's office alone.

Three

This is what happened. Last Thursday, Karen and Amy and I were supposed to have PE at eleven. We're in a modern-dance class with a lot of seventh-graders. We like the class. Miss Steadman is a good teacher and we have interesting assignments, like choreographing our own dances in teams and dancing them for the rest of the class.

But Thursday, after we had gone through all the fuss of changing into leotards, we went into the gym and nobody was there. Then Miss Steadman came in wearing her regular clothes.

"Oh, I'm sorry, girls," she said. "Didn't anyone tell you? All the seventh-graders have been called out for an assembly about testing. I'm supposed to go to it, too. So, look—why don't you limber up a bit with some exercises and then go spend the rest of the period in the library?"

That sounded like fun, just the three of us in the

empty gym. We began to run around crazily, half dancing, half playing tag. Karen raced off with her arms spread out, yelling, "Up, up in the sky—it's a bird, it's a plane, it's Wonder Woman!" She looked like it, too. Karen is five feet eleven inches tall but she's very easy and graceful with her body. I'm the type of person who is always bumping and tripping into things. I have never in my life been able to do a whole cartwheel. Now Karen was turning cartwheels straight across the gym. Amy and I ran up to each other, pulled out imaginary canes, tipped our top hats, and strutted out toward the basket arm in arm.

"Wait for me!" Karen yelled, and she ran up and broke in between us. We two-stepped down to the back of the gym. When we got there we leaned back in a great bow of triumph with our arms bent out toward our imaginary audience.

"Listen to them cheer," Amy said.

"While we smile modestly," said Karen.

"I'm starving!" I said.

"Tough," said Amy. "So am I, but the cafeteria's closed."

"Oh, let's go out to The Break," Karen said. "Nobody knows where we're supposed to be, and it's half an hour till next period."

The Coffee Break, and the one-block hill you walk down to get to it, are off limits to Camden students. So is practically everything around our school except the blacktop area in back where the buses park, and the football field, and the track. There's some grass between the junior high and the senior high, but we're not supposed to sit there, even in good weather. It gives you a really caged-in feeling to stay inside school all the time. Maybe that's why people are always cutting. But I never did before. If you get caught cutting, even the first time, you get suspended. Some kids just take that chance, but I've always been scared to. I worry about what people would say. It's the Aunt Rose side of me. My parents would die, I know that.

That's what I'm worrying about now. Now that it's too late.

But last Thursday it seemed so natural to duck out for juice and a doughnut. Running around the gym had made us feel silly and free, and we weren't really expected in the library—and we were hungry.

So we left. Karen said that if anyone stopped us we should say we were on an errand for Miss Steadman to buy coffee for the PE teachers. That didn't seem like a very good excuse to me so I was glad we could go out by the gym door. There usually aren't any hall monitors there. Once we were out of the building it wasn't so scary. I tried to look like somebody who had to meet their mother in the parking lot and go to the dentist, or somebody who got excused to pick up their little brother at Kennedy Elementary. The three of us walked along slowly, enjoying the sun and air. I was trying not to think about cutting school.

Amy said, "It's such a stupid rule, anyway."

Karen said, "At least at boarding school you can walk around outdoors when you want to."

"Look at the willow color," I said. It was still too early for real spring, but you could see the willows turning yellow. I always love how they look.

We walked into The Break, and we got caught.

Would you believe that three teachers were sitting there drinking coffee? One of them was Mr. Drury, my math teacher. Dreary Drury. "What are you girls doing here?" he demanded.

"Well, we didn't have our regular gym class so we came down for doughnuts," I said. I forgot about saying we were on an errand for Miss Steadman.

"We don't have to be anywhere for half an hour," Karen added.

"That isn't the issue," said Mr. Drury. "The point is, you are off school grounds and I'll have to report you. Give me your names."

I once read about a little kid who thought he had given his whole self away when a policeman took his name. When I told Mr. Drury my name—for heaven's sake, he ought to *know* my name, I've been in his math class all semester—I felt that way. It was as though he had taken part of *me* along with it.

Karen and Amy gave their names. The two women teachers with Mr. Drury stared at us. You would think they could have shown some human sympathy. After all, they had felt like leaving school, too.

Mr. Drury told us to go back and report to the office. "Make it quick," he said. "This is serious, you know. You kids never think about consequences. Cutting means suspension."

Suspension! This was the first time I really believed it would happen.

We walked back to school fast. Everybody in the office was busy. Finally a woman at the front desk looked up.

"Yes, girls?"

"We're supposed to tell you we were away from school, at The Break," Karen said.

"Well, were you?"

"Yes," I said, "But—"

"Never mind the buts," the woman said. "Cutting is cutting. I'll have to report you to Mr. Gross. But he can't see you—he's away at a conference this week. Maybe Mr. Gottsegen will talk to you, but I doubt that he has the time today. You'll just have to go on to your next class and wait to hear from us."

We went out. The bell hadn't rung yet, so we went to wait in the girl's bathroom. I hate it in there. It's always full of cigarette smoke so you can hardly breathe. The sinks and toilets are stopped up with paper towels. It's disgusting.

"Anyway," said Amy, "we got away from school for ten minutes."

"Do you think we really will get suspended?" I asked.

"Of course not, dopey," Karen said. "They never suspend you the first time. They just try to scare you, that's all." But she didn't sound very sure.

"Do they tell your parents?" I asked.

"I don't know," said Karen. "But who cares? My

parents think the school rules are stupid. They wouldn't *let* this school suspend me."

"I sure hope they don't do it, though," Amy said. "My parents would kill me."

"Yeah, my parents would really be upset too," I said.

We went on to our classes, and at the end of the day we met in the hall. Nothing had happened. We hadn't been called down to the office.

"Maybe they forgot," I said.

"Never," said Amy. "They don't forget down there. They just haven't got around to us yet."

Karen ran out because her bus was leaving. "Safe till tomorrow," she yelled back.

But I didn't feel safe, and I haven't felt safe since then. On Friday, we all got notes from the office telling us to come to Mr. Gottsegen's office Monday morning. The notes said that suspension is the automatic punishment for leaving school during school hours, and that we would be suspended.

That was what I had been worrying about all weekend—that on top of Mom's housecleaning work. How could I do such a thing to my family at a time like this?

I really don't think what we did was so awful. But why did I let myself do it when I *knew* it could get me suspended? If only we hadn't gone to The Break! For one measly doughnut that I never even got, I brought this trouble on my parents and this awful guilty feeling on myself.

I just want to go somewhere and yell, "I didn't mean to. I really didn't mean to!"

Four

Karen and Amy were sitting on the bench in the office where you wait for appointments. They looked sort of formal and stiff, like people I didn't know. They said "Hi," and pushed over for me, and I sat down. We didn't talk.

The usual morning rush was going on. Kids were showing excuses for absence or asking for early dismissal passes. Office workers were answering telephones and rushing into the mimeograph room. Substitutes were checking in and teachers were setting up appointments. The school clock clicked, the mimeograph went thunk, thunk, and one poor kid kept arguing with the woman at the front desk. "But, honest, I didn't know I had to have a written note and nobody's home and the orchestra's leaving at 1:30 and I have this eight-bar solo in the middle of the first piece!"

"All right, girls, let's hear your problem," said Mrs. Vogel, who is Mr. Gottsegen's secretary.

Karen told her we were supposed to see Mr. Gottsegen because we went off school grounds last week.

"He's in conference," Mrs. Vogel said. "I don't think he really has to see you, anyway. He'll just send your suspension letters to your parents." She looked at us crossly. "Is this the first infraction?"

We nodded.

"OK, then, let's keep it simple. No need to bother Mr. Gottsegen. Tell me your names again."

She wrote down Karen's and Amy's, but when I said mine she looked surprised. "Are you related to Julia Myers?"

"She's my sister."

"Well, I'm surprised to hear that. Julia was an outstanding student all through junior high."

I nodded. I never know whether I'm supposed to thank people for saying good things about Julia, or apologize for myself.

Mrs. Vogel tore the sheet with our names off her pad. "OK, girls, that's it. Go along to your classes."

We stood there. Mrs. Vogel turned away to her desk. I had to find out what would happen next, so I went after her and touched her elbow.

"Mrs. Vogel?"

"What?" she demanded.

"When will the letter come?" I asked.

"It'll come when it comes," Mrs. Vogel said. "I can't predict how the post office works. I'll mail the letters out tonight. Now go along or you'll be marked down for cutting another class."

You know how in books they say that someone felt

weak in their stomach from fear? I felt weak in the stomach from fear.

Karen and Amy stood in the office doorway. They looked serious.

"Well, it won't kill us," Karen said. "It's only a letter."

"My parents will kill *me* when they get it," Amy said. "They'll be so mad they'll make me stay in the house for weeks for punishment. I know they will."

"My parents are going to feel so bad," I said. "This will just seem awful to them. Especially after Julia. They'll act like it's the end of the world. I won't be able to explain to them that lots of people get suspended, that it happens all the time. And wait till my Aunt Rose hears! She won't ever let me forget it."

This will prove to Aunt Rose that I'm going to turn out bad, the way she always knew I would. She'll be convinced that if I had only stood up straight and taken a little pride in my appearance the way she said, it wouldn't have happened. Oh, wow. I don't know how my parents stand having Aunt Rose second-guess everything that happens in our family.

The warning bell rang. We were going to be late. We cut out of the office and started to run down the hall.

A hall monitor darted out of a doorway.

"Where do you think you're going in such a hurry? Slow down or I'll report you."

People always seem to talk like that in our school: "Hurry up." "Slow down." "Get going." "Wait a minute."

At least Karen and I had Mrs. Inman first period. She's a good teacher. She likes kids. The class is called human relations and we talk about interesting things. The only problem is that George Waldman is in the class and so are his friends, Jimmy Rizzo and Bernie Muller. I wish they weren't. I think they signed up because they thought it would be an easy class, and they couldn't get out of it when they found out it involved work. Sometimes it seems sort of funny that I can't even relate to some of the humans in my human relations class.

Diane Johnson was giving a report on employment in Camden Woods. She said that over seventy percent of employed people in Camden Woods work out of town, in the city. There is one factory out on the parkway and one over in Mayfield, but the only other work is in small stores and services.

"How many people in this class have a parent or parents who work in the city?" asked Mrs. Inman.

All but four kids raised their hands. I was one who didn't and George Waldman was another. George's father used to work in the liquor store, but now I think he lives in Florida. When we talked about city helpers in grade school, George always used to raise his hand and say, "My father's a store man!" I did, too. It's funny how your ideas change when you grow up. Most little kids would love to work in a store or carry mail or drive a bus. But when you get to be my age, you suddenly find out that some people think it's much more important to be a banker or a doctor.

George Waldman and Bernie Muller were snickering in the back of the room. Diane Johnson looked uncomfortable. I know how that feels. She was probably wondering if her shirt had come unbuttoned or her fly was unzipped. It seems as though George and people like him are always sitting in the back of schoolrooms, snickering and chewing gum and making what you know must be dirty jokes about girls in the class or the teacher. Teachers mostly yell at them or try to ignore them. But Mrs. Inman always talks to them the same as to other people. She doesn't seem to see that George Waldman is really disgusting. Sometimes I wish I could go to a boarding school, where I bet everybody would be more—you know—smart and interested, and nobody would laugh and snicker in the back of the room. Still, I don't know. They'd probably be stuck-up.

Mrs. Inman said, "Listen, George, you're going to have to give a report soon. So you ought to pay better attention to how other people do it."

"I don't have any topic," George said, laughing at Jimmy Rizzo.

"Why don't you come by after school and talk about it," said Mrs. Inman. "Anyone else? How about you, Cathy? We've hardly talked at all this semester."

She's so nice. She tries to get to know everyone, not just the A students. But I just couldn't talk to her today. I wonder if she knew about the suspension. It would be awful to have to talk to her about that, in front of George.

"I have to take the early bus today," I said.

"Well, stop by as soon as you can," Mrs. Inman said. "I'll expect you today, then, George. OK?"

Bernie poked George and snorted at that, but George didn't laugh. "OK, see ya," he told Mrs. Inman.

The bell rang.

I still hadn't told my friends about Mom's work. It just seemed too hard to explain, especially when I was already feeling bad. But I kept thinking about Mom. Like when I saw the janitor pushing his cart with the mop and buckets down the hall. Most of the time we hardly even notice him. But he might be some kid's father. I hoped the people Mom was working for were nice. I wondered if she was supposed to clean out their toilets.

At lunch, Karen kept talking about her horse. Usually I like to hear about Willie, but today all I could think about was how expensive it is to have a horse. Karen doesn't seem to notice the way she talks about money, as though everyone had it.

"Willie needs a new saddle," she said. "His old saddle is so worn it cuts into him."

"How much does a saddle cost?" Amy asked.

"About two hundred dollars," Karen said. "I'll have to use the birthday money I put away, and some allowances, and ask my father for the rest."

"Will he give it to you?" asked Amy.

"Oh, sure," Karen said. "He'll complain about it, but he'll cough it up."

Chris came over to the table. "Want to come over this afternoon, Cathy?" he asked.

"I can't," I said. "I told Mom I'd go right home." I had said I'd make supper for the family, because Julia had to work late at the yearbook office.

The bell rang. Lunch period was over.

"See ya around," Chris said.

I stacked my dishes and started toward the clearing counter.

"Look where you're going, dope," some boy said, and he pushed into me and bumped my tray. One of my dirty dishes fell off and broke. Everybody in the cafeteria stopped talking and stared at me. I don't know why people think it's funny when something like that happens, but a lot of kids laughed. I picked up the pieces. I was not going to cry. Crying in school is the worst.

"Be a little careful, you kids," a kitchen lady said to me. As though it was my fault! The kitchen ladies are like the hall monitors—they act as though you're their kid. At least Mom didn't get a job as a school aide at my school. That would have been horrible. I never even thought of that!

The day finally ended. The early bus, the one that leaves five minutes after the bell rings, is always extra noisy. Kids were screaming and throwing apples and leftover pieces of sandwich. I couldn't even think. I just sat and waited for the ride to end.

But the afternoon bus driver is nice. He talks to all the kids. When I got off, he said, "Well, now, that does it for today, I guess. Have yourself a good afternoon."

"Same to you," I told him. It's amazing how much better you feel when just one person treats you pleasantly.

The house was quiet when I unlocked the door and went in. I was glad to be the only one at home. I made

27

myself a cup of tea and took it up to my room and turned on the radio and lay down. I cried some, and that felt good. Then I closed my eyes to relax for just a minute. I must have dozed off right away.

Five

That's me. On the one day I wanted to do everything right—cook the dinner and set the table before Mom came home—I fell asleep. Luckily, I woke up in time to make it because Sneaky Pete, the disc jockey I listen to, came on suddenly after a record yelling, "All right, boys and girls, everybody up, time to rock and roll!" I don't know why he said that at four-thirty in the afternoon, but he certainly got me up.

I rushed downstairs and pulled things out of the refrigerator and began to mix up a meat loaf. I scrubbed potatoes and put everything into the oven fast. By the time Mom got home it had begun to smell like dinner. I was glad I had managed to do that much, because she looked awfully tired when she pushed open the door slowly and came in. She sat down at the kitchen table with her coat still on and set her pocketbook in front of her.

"Well, let's see what I got for it," she said, pulling

a roll of dollars from her change purse. "Sixteen dollars and carfare, that's what I got."

I put the kettle on for tea. "What's carfare?"

"That's one of the extras that's supposed to make housework worthwhile. They pay your way there and back. Of course, they still had to pick me up at the end of the bus line, because the house was so far out. It must have been near Karen's."

That made me feel sort of funny.

"Another extra," Mom went on, "is that people sometimes give you leftovers from dinner parties and clothes they don't want, things like that."

"That's disgusting," I said, pouring water over a tea bag for Mom. "They ought to give you more money for doing such hard work."

"It's hard, all right," Mom said in a stiff voice, as though she was trying to sound matter-of-fact and not sorry for herself. "I vacuumed every room in that house —it's fourteen big ones—and mopped the bathrooms— that's three bathrooms—and polished the handles on all the antique furniture, and I don't even want to guess how many *that* was. All the time Mrs. Thomas kept following me around saying, 'Clara, did you notice that little place behind the chest where the dust collects,' or, 'Clara—'"

"She calls you *Clara*?" I interrupted.

"Sure," said Mom. "Why not?"

"What did you call her?"

" 'Mrs. Thomas.' That's her name."

"Well, your name is Mrs. Myers, for goodness' sake. Doesn't she know that?"

"Of course she knows, hon. Now don't get all upset over that. When you go to do housework, people call you by your first name. They don't mean anything by it."

I think that it is just disgusting for anyone to call a woman of my mother's age "Clara" unless they are her friend or a relative or something. What right did this Mrs. Thomas have to act superior to my mother? Mom is every bit as good as she is, and she probably works about ten times harder. Just wait till I tell Dad, I thought. He won't like that.

"Now, I don't want you to go on about that to your Dad, Catherine," Mom said. "All this is hard enough on him without you bothering him about names. You have to learn not to get so excited over every little thing. There's enough terrible things wrong in this world for you not to waste energy on unimportant ones."

"Yeah, well, tell that to Aunt Rose sometime," I said. "Unimportant things are her specialty."

"Catherine!" Mom said. Then she laughed. "Thank goodness Rose isn't here to hear me complain like this. She'd be sure to say 'I told you so.'"

"You *should* complain, Mom," I said. "I think it's awful that you have to work so hard."

"Hard work is not awful," Mom said firmly. "Millions of people work as hard or harder every day of their lives, without anybody to make a fuss over them."

That's a thing about Mom. She just won't feel sorry for herself. She always thinks about somebody worse-off than her. When I'm feeling bad, I don't want to hear about worse-off people.

"How was school today, Cathy?" Mom asked.

"OK, I guess," I said. If she only knew! Mom wants so badly for me to do well in school. It isn't that she expects me to be just like Julia—she really doesn't. But she wants me to behave well and work hard and make good grades and go to college and be somebody. And I have to go and get myself suspended. Mom's going to feel so bad!

"The meat loaf won't be done for half an hour, Mom," I said, "and Dad and Julia won't be home before that. Why don't you go upstairs and lie down for a while?"

"Oh, Cathy, I couldn't!" Mom said. "If I lay down for one minute I think I'd fall right off for the whole night. But I tell you what, I'll let you finish up out here and set the table and all, and I'll go read the paper in the living room like a lady."

When Mom said that, it just made me want to cry.

"You *are* a lady, Mom," I said, hugging her as she walked into the living room.

Mom sat down in the big chair and pulled me into it with her, half on her lap and half beside her. She brushed my hair with her hand and kissed me on the cheek. Then she leaned back with her arm around me.

"Catherine, you are a very big help to me," she said. "You don't know how nice it was to come in all tired out and smell that meat loaf cooking. Now, I won't want to ask you to do that every day, but it makes me feel very good tonight."

I sat up and looked at Mom. "Thanks for going to work and everything," I said. I really meant it. It is a loving thing for Mom to go and clean other people's houses so our family will have more money.

Mom said, "Now, scoot. It's pretty hard to read my paper with a big girl like you on my lap."

I went back to the kitchen and set out plates and glasses. I was cutting up the salad when Julia came in.

"Smells good," she said. "Is Mom home?"

"In the living room," I said.

Julia went in to Mom. "How was it?"

"All right," Mom said. "Now that I know what it's like, I won't worry about it so much."

"Was it a nice house?"

"Not as nice as this one, I'll tell you that."

"Oh, Mom, you'd say that about the White House!" Julia laughed.

"I probably would," said Mom.

Julia came back to the kitchen. "You should see Nathan's new pictures," she said. "He developed them today. They're terrific. Mr. Altman says this will be the best yearbook he's ever seen. We're lucky to have him for advisor. He makes good suggestions, but he lets us do it. Did you know he used to work on a newspaper, before he was a teacher? I'm learning a lot about writing from him."

"I suppose you're going to end up being a great author, too," I said, only halfway joking.

"No, I'm not," Julia said, as though she had thought about it but decided not to. "I love that feeling, though, when you say just what you want to say, just right."

I wish I knew that feeling.

The car turned into the driveway.

"Here's Dad," I called to Mom.

Julia ran out to meet him. They came in the door together.

"Hi, Dad," I said. I gave him a butterfly kiss on the nose, the way I used to when I was little.

"Hello, Catherine," said Dad, smiling at me. "Smells pretty darn good in here. You the cook?"

"Yep," I said.

"That's a nice help to your mother," he said. "Where is she?"

"I'm in here, Bob," Mom called.

Dad went to her. "How did it go, Clara?"

"It wasn't that bad, Bob, it really wasn't. Now that I've done it once, it seems pretty straightforward. I don't think I'll have any trouble getting used to it."

"I hope they appreciated your work," Dad said.

"Well," Mom laughed, "they didn't come right out and say I was the best cleaning lady they ever had. But then again, they didn't make any complaints. I suppose they don't care too much, one way or the other, as long as the work gets done."

"Well, *I* say they're pretty lucky to get you," Dad told her. He hung up his sweater in the hall.

"Bob," Mom said, "Come on and sit down here and take this paper. I'm just on my way upstairs to comb my hair and wash up before we eat. Catherine's done all the cooking."

Everybody likes the big chair best, the one she'd been sitting in. But we all try to give it to Dad when he comes home from work.

34

"Stay there, Clara," Dad said. "I've already looked at the paper at the store."

"Now, Bob, I know you didn't have time to read it, closing up and all. Take it. I'm going upstairs."

I saw Dad touch Mom's arm as she went past. Then he sat down in the chair and began to read the paper.

At dinner Julia talked about the yearbook. I could tell how proud Mom and Dad were.

"You're certainly working very hard on it, Julia," Dad said. "Dave Burden stopped in for coffee today and he said, 'I hear your daughter's editing the Camden High yearbook.' He seemed to be pretty impressed with that."

"Well, lots of people help," Julia said. "Especially Nathan. The only bad thing is, we're working against a deadline and some of the kids who signed up last fall dropped out when the dull stuff like proofreading came along. There's an awful lot left to do and I get scared we won't make it."

"Could I help out?" I asked. "Even if I'm not in high school?"

"Well, sure, Cath, I don't see why not," Julia said. "Would you really like to?"

"Yeah, I would," I said. And I realized when I said it that I really would. It would be fun to go next door to the high school and see the inside of the yearbook office. And help out. "Thanks, Julia."

"How's school, Catherine?" Dad asked.

"Pretty good," I said. Pretty awful, I should have said.

"Any problems?" Dad asked. People always seem to ask questions like that when you don't want to answer them.

"Not really," I said. I hate to lie to my father. "I have this report to do for social studies, and I don't know what topic. But I'll think of one."

"Make sure you get down to it soon," Dad said.

"You don't want to fall behind," Mom added.

Julia and I cleaned up after dinner. We decided that I'd start working at the yearbook next week after school. I could take the late bus home. I didn't tell Julia why I didn't want to start this week. The thing was, I had to look for the mail before anyone else got home. I had to know when the suspension letter came. My whole future seemed to be tied up with the U.S. Postal Service.

Six

The letter didn't come the next day, or the next. Each time I looked through the mail and didn't find it, I was relieved. But only for a minute. It was like when the dentist cancels your appointment—at first you get this great sensation of freedom, but then you realize you just have to wait longer for the awful day to come.

Two days later I had to decide once and for all what project to do for my human relations class. I knew I should have stayed after to talk to Mrs. Inman, but each afternoon I avoided it. I didn't have any ideas to talk about, and I was ashamed to say so. I wished somebody would just give me some idea. Like Julia.

"But if I suggested something to you, it wouldn't be the same," Julia said while we waited for the bus. "The idea is for you to figure out a project that needs doing, and then do it."

"Yeah, but like what?" I said.

"I don't know," Julia said. "The whole point is for

you to think something up. You're lucky. When I was in eighth grade we had to write things like 'Why I Am Proud to Be an American' for social studies. They didn't even have a human relations class then, and I never heard about doing research. People *told* us things, they never asked us to find out for ourselves. You're getting a much better start for college."

"What if I don't want to go to college?"

"Oh, Cath." Julia sort of shook me, smiling. "You're so nutty. You'll want to when the time comes."

"Don't be too sure," I said. "It just may be that I won't."

"But then, how are you going to learn to be something, like a scientist or a teacher?"

"If I don't even know what I want to be, how can I go to college to learn about it?" I asked. "That's the whole thing that gets me confused."

Julia said, "Listen. Just wait. Don't worry. You don't have to decide everything right now. You have time."

I know I have it. I just don't seem to know how to use it very well.

I tried to think up a project on the bus, but nothing came to me. George Waldman didn't help. He kept poking his knees into the back of my seat and humming under his breath. When we went past women waiting for the city bus, George rapped on the window and said things they couldn't hear: "Hey, baby, going my way?" or "My, my, honey, want a ride?" On the way out of the bus, he pressed next to me and whispered, "Got your project? You want some help?"

I got away from him as fast as I could. But when the first bell rang I couldn't make myself go to human relations. I felt too dumb. Suddenly, on the way down the hall, I decided I would go to the nurse instead.

I met Karen outside the nurse's office.

"What's the matter?" she said.

"I feel sort of sick," I said. "Tell Mrs. Inman."

The nurse's office is one of the grimmest rooms in our school. It smells of alcohol and gym socks and the last traces of vomit. Somebody is always talking on the phone in a croupy whisper, and there is always a kid stretched out on the cot, with one arm dangling down.

Mrs. Foster pulled a thermometer out of a boy's mouth when I came in, looked at it and then at me.

"What's the trouble?" she asked. Pleasantly. There is nothing wrong with Mrs. Foster, it's just the environment she works in that's depressing. The only decoration on the walls is an eye chart.

"I don't feel good," I said. "Can I lie down in here this period?"

"Where are you supposed to be now?" Mrs. Foster asked.

"Social studies—human relations, with Mrs. Inman."

"Can you afford to miss it? I suppose you ought to, if you really feel bad. But then, maybe you ought to be home in bed. Can we reach your mother?"

"She works," I said.

"Can we phone her?" asked Mrs. Foster. "I think she ought to know you don't feel good."

"Well, see, I don't know her number," I said.

"What company does she work for?" Mrs. Foster asked. "We can look it up."

"She doesn't work for a company," I said. Everybody in the room, sick or not, was listening. "She works for different people."

"How do you mean, different people?" Mrs. Foster demanded. "*Which* different people?" She wasn't trying to be mean. I just wasn't being very helpful.

"You could call my father," I said, "At Bob's Newspaper Store, downtown."

"Is Bob Myers your father?" Mrs. Foster asked. "He's a great person. I get my paper in there every afternoon."

That was nice. She called him up and had this friendly conversation. "He thinks your mother is working for a Mrs. Stanton today," she said after she hung up. "Do you know where that would be?"

"Oh, yes, that's way over by the state line," I said. "I guess I just ought to lie here awhile and see how I feel, if that's OK?"

"Be my guest," said Mrs. Foster. "You do look flushed and tired. Do you have a sore throat or a stuffy nose?"

"I don't think so," I said. "I just feel exhausted." Which was true. I *was* exhausted, from all my worrying. I was as tired as if I had flu.

I pulled up the blanket Mrs. Foster gave me—it was gray and scratchy like all nurse's office blankets—and began to relax. It felt good to lie there without any responsibilities. I was almost dozing off when sputters on the PA system woke me up.

Attention please, students and teachers. To-night's home baseball game will be played at 7:30 instead of 8:00. That's 7:30, on the home field. Let's go Tigers!

There was more static and then the band came over the speaker playing the "Camden March," which is really "On, Wisconsin" with the words changed to "On, Oh Camden." I hate our PA system. It's so unfair that just one person in the office has the power to inter-rupt hundreds of people all over the school. It's like "Sleeping Beauty." Everybody stops what they're doing —with their theorems unproved or their free throw never thrown or their poems unfinished—while this mysterious voice holds them in its spell.

I couldn't get back to dozing because the tune of "On, Oh Camden" was in my head. I always get stuck with tunes I hear, like television commercials or band songs or little kids' piano pieces. Once I hear some song, I keep on singing it all day long in my head, with what-ever I'm thinking about for words. Like, "Buy some toothpaste, buy some toothpaste" for "On, Oh Camden." Or, for example, to the start of Beethoven's Fifth Sym-phony, "It looks like rain." Once I get going, I can't seem to stop. "It looks like ray,ay,ain, it looks like ray, ay,ain, it looks like ray, ay, *ain*."

But after a while I did go to sleep. Even with the bells and the telephone and people coming in and out of the nurse's office.

At lunch time, Mrs. Foster sent down to the cafeteria for some soup. I ate mine and went back off.

I woke up at the end of the day with a voice saying, "You are dismissed," over the loudspeaker, and the band playing "The Battle Hymn of the Republic" through the static. All these pieces are on a record that the band made. The school office and people in the band are the only ones who bought it.

Other kids in the nurse's office were sitting up and putting on their sneakers and collecting their books. Mrs. Foster smiled at us. "Feel better," she said. "Go home and get some sleep."

I walked out to my locker, looking for Karen. I wanted to see if she'd come home with me. I thought I could tell her about Mom's work easier if she came to my house. I was tired of not telling anybody. Holding things in is exhausting. At least I could talk about the suspension with Karen and Amy. It would be awful to be suspended alone.

I was working my combination when someone ran up behind me. "Catherine."

I turned around. It was Mrs. Inman.

"We missed you this morning," she said. "Karen told me you didn't feel well. So I'm glad to catch you now. I knew you'd want to get started on your project. What have you decided to work on?"

I really felt sick then. Mrs. Inman stood right in front of me, smiling. People rushed past us, yelling and slamming locker doors and running out for the bus. I wonder if Mrs. Inman knew how guilty I felt. She didn't seem to be accusing me at all, just trying to help.

I blurted out, "Mrs. Inman, I really want to get started on a project, but the thing is, I haven't even figured out what to do yet. I don't seem to have any ideas!"

"That's one of the worst things about any assignment, isn't it," Mrs. Inman said, "when you aren't sure what you really want to do."

"Yeah, really."

"I've noticed," she said, "that the best projects in human relations are the ones where kids work on topics close to them. Things that are on their mind."

"I have a lot of things on my mind," I said. I almost told her about the suspension, right then, but at the last minute I didn't. "Like, my sister already knows what kind of work she wants to do and I don't. And, well, my mother just began to work, and she didn't have any experience and so the best job she could get was housework."

"She didn't have any experience at all?" Mrs. Inman asked.

"Not the kind that counts," I said. "She fixes everything in our house and things like that. And she used to be a volunteer reading helper at Allen School. But they don't have any money for aides there."

"Don't I know it," Mrs. Inman said. "Teachers in this district are already getting the lowest salaries in our part of the state. And there's no money for aides in the lower grades."

"Mom had one little boy at Allen School who was

just beginning to read because she helped him," I said. "But she probably won't be able to work there anymore, because she won't have time."

"That's the trouble with volunteer work," Mrs. Inman said. "People can't afford to do it. I think it's a shame that someone like your mother can't earn money for useful work like that. And it's hard luck for those kids at Allen School when their reading program gets cut back."

"I know it," I said.

Then Mrs. Inman and I seemed to have the same idea at the same time. I honestly don't know whether it was mine or hers, but she says it doesn't matter. The idea is that I'm going to see if kids from my school could go down and tutor kids at Allen School.

Mrs. Inman thought they might let people work down there during study periods. Or maybe after school. Anyway, I'm going to go to Allen School and talk to Mrs. Pflaum, the teacher my mother worked with. Then I'll have to talk to people at my school. Mrs. Inman wants me to talk to Mr. Gottsegen. That's the only problem. I didn't tell Mrs. Inman about the suspension, and I certainly don't feel like going in and talking to Mr. Gottsegen right now. I wonder if he would even let someone like me arrange a project with little kids. Maybe he would think I wasn't good enough. I just hate waiting for this horrible suspension to happen. I wish the letter would come so I could get it all over with!

Seven

It came.

The same afternoon I talked to Mrs. Inman. When I got home and opened the mailbox, I saw the letter—a long envelope with an addressograph label that said MRMRSMYERS, like all school mail. I wished this letter was about a school board election or the spring concert. But in another way I was almost glad that it was finally my suspension letter, here at last.

I put the mail on the front-hall table. Then I went upstairs and cleaned my room and came back down and took out the garbage and swept the kitchen floor. I didn't want to forget anything like that on this day. Then I began to cut up onions and brown the meat for a spaghetti sauce.

I wondered whether Mom or Julia would come home first. I wished all over again that I'd told Julia about the suspension. Now everyone will know at once. I thought about what they'd probably say.

My mother will say, "Oh, *Cathy*." I just die of shame when she says that. It's all she needs to say.

Dad will say something like, "This is very serious, Catherine. It isn't like you to get into trouble." He always thinks I'm perfect.

I don't know what Julia will say. Suddenly I felt really mad at Julia. She'll probably say something like, "What did you go and do a dopey thing like that for?"

She always acts so superior. Why am I the one who always looks bad? I never asked to have this marvelous, perfect sister. I just got born and there she was. Sometimes I wish I never even had a sister. Nobody understands how hard it is to be me.

When I put the spaghetti into boiling water, some drops splashed up and hit me on the cheek. My face hurt and my feelings hurt. I ran to the front room and put my face down on a cool couch pillow and cried.

Naturally, I was still crying when a car turned into the driveway. Naturally, it was Aunt Rose's car. She must have met Mom at the bus stop. That made the day about one hundred and forty percent awful.

I ran upstairs to the bathroom and ran cold water onto a washcloth and pressed it over my eyes. I brushed my hair and tucked in my shirt and told myself, "Take it easy. Act natural. Smile." I smiled into the mirror. My reflection looked like a girl smiling. How could I look like that when I was so scared inside?

Mom called, "Are you there, Cathy?"

"Yup, coming," I said. I went downstairs.

"There's the cook," Aunt Rose said. "Smells like something's boiling over on the stove, better go check."

46

Mom was looking through the mail. "How are you, hon?" she asked. She pulled out the school letter.

"OK, Mom," I said, and ran into the kitchen to look at the pots. Nothing was boiling over. I stayed anyhow. I just couldn't face Mom and Aunt Rose together. I started to wash the lettuce.

Aunt Rose followed me into the kitchen, took off her coat and sat down. "Aren't you going to offer me a cup of tea?" she asked. She looked at me hard. "Do you know you're all blotchy and red in the face? I hope you aren't getting some allergy. Those things are the devil to clean up. Denise had spots on her scalp for months, back when she was four, maybe five—no, four, I'm sure, because she wasn't in school yet. We tried I don't know how many creams and salves, but none of them worked. Poor Denise, the spots itched her something awful. She used to cry nights. I had to slap her hands every time she tried to scratch. Those allergies are terrible. Thank you, Catherine, now if you could spare me a little sugar and some cream—or some milk, if that's all you have."

I set them out.

"Clara!" called Aunt Rose. "Aren't you going to have some tea with me? You're not being very sociable!"

Mom came into the kitchen. She gave me a look so sad and hurt and tired that I couldn't look back. I had to turn away to the stove. I put the tea bag in Mom's cup and poured water into it. Then I set it in front of her. Mom had her elbow on the table and her face in her hand.

"Thank you, Catherine," she said.

"You're welcome, Mom," I said.

"Clara, running around like this is going to be the death of you," said Aunt Rose. "Taking care of other people's houses, too tired to care for your own."

"Goodness, Rose," Mom said. "Does this place look uncared for?"

"Well, no, but it doesn't take much to see you're already dragging yourself around. And the girls will have the burden of it. Between you and Bob's hours there won't be a parent in the house most of the time. With the girls the age they are, you're just asking for trouble."

"Oh, Rose, I'm too tired to go into it now."

"And that's another thing. Tired, exhausted, and what have you got to show for it? Not more than two dollars, two twenty-five an hour. That's more than plenty for those others, the shiftless kind who won't do a lick of work. . . ."

Mom raised her head. "*What* others?"

"You know," Aunt Rose said. "You can't trust one of *them* to give you an honest hour's work for an hour's fair pay. The papers are full of complaints. Those people come out here expecting something for nothing, and then when a respectable person like you comes along you don't even get a fair deal."

"Oh, Rose, you don't understand, you really don't," Mom said. "Today on the bus I met a lady, Mrs. Johnson, who rides all the way out from the city to do housework. She told me she can't find decent housing anywhere in Camden Woods for what she could afford, so she has to leave her two little boys at seven in the morning and not get back to them till near seven at

48

night. Worrying about them all the time she's cleaning house. And then people get mad if she won't stay on an extra hour at the last minute, or they won't give her more carfare money when the bus fare goes up. It's a terrible thing," Mom said.

"Things are tight all over," Aunt Rose said.

"Yes," said Mom. "Although some of the places I've been, 'tight' means letting the gardener go, and not much more."

I drained the spaghetti, trying to catch the slippery pieces before they slid over the edge of the drainer into the sink.

Mom said, "This Mrs. Johnson said some of the women were going to get together in a houseworkers' group. Have one phone number to call for all the women and set a fair wage, the same for everybody. Ask for vacations and sick leave."

"Sounds crazy to me," Aunt Rose said. "You watch, those people'll talk themselves out of any work at all. They'll find out soon enough. You can't get something for nothing."

"Oh, Rose," said Mom, pushing away her cup of tea and getting up. "I just don't have the heart to argue with you tonight."

Aunt Rose got up too. "Now, Clara, I'm not arguing. Just speaking my mind. But I'm going to go along and leave you now. It's time to get back and cook up Denise's chop."

Denise has a lamb chop, with green peas and mashed potatoes, every single night. That's all she'll eat.

"Denise will be wondering where I am," Aunt Rose

said. "I told her I'd be right home after I went to the store, but when I saw you get off that bus I just couldn't leave you to walk home. It's a pity Bob can't close up early enough to meet you."

"Yes," Mom said. "Thanks for the ride, Rose. It was a help."

I could hardly wait for Aunt Rose to go, but I was scared of being alone with Mom, too. Aunt Rose stood in the doorway twisting her key chain on her finger and telling Mom the best brand of upholstery shampoo. I hung around the kitchen setting out plates, filling glasses, folding napkins. Feeling awful.

At last the door slammed shut. Mom came into the kitchen with her pocketbook and put it on the table in front of her. She opened it and pulled out the suspension letter.

"What I just can't understand is," she said heavily, as though we had been talking about it since she first got home, "why did you do it? Why?"

"I don't know, Mom," I said. "I only wish I hadn't. You don't know how much I wish it."

"Wishes don't make it so," Mom said. "It's too late for wishes now."

"I know it," I said.

"Oh, Cathy," Mom said, sighing. "How did it happen? How could you be so thoughtless of all of us? It makes me so ashamed, getting this letter. I don't know how I'll hold my head up. My own daughter, suspended!"

"It didn't seem so bad at the time," I told her.

Mom flared up. "Well, it seems plenty bad enough

right now, I'll tell you that. And it's going to seem worse when you have to tell your father. This is just going to kill your father. As if he didn't have enough on his mind right now, with me going to work and his business dropping off and his costs going up. And now this—"

"I didn't know his business was that bad, Mom."

"You didn't know because your father doesn't talk about it all the time. He tries to keep his worries to himself. Keeps it all bottled in. He's half sick now, waiting for Julia's college letters to come. What he'll do when he hears this, I don't know."

"Oh, Mom."

"Never mind, 'Oh, Mom,' now," Mom said. "It's too late for that." Suddenly she pushed away from the table and came behind me and shook my shoulders, hard. "You're suspended. Suspended! Oh, Cathy, you make me so mad—"

Julia opened the back door and stopped. "Mom! What's the matter?"

Mom let go of me. "Cathy has gotten herself suspended, that's what's the matter."

"Oh, no!" said Julia. "Is it true?" she asked me.

"Yes," I said. I just wished I could explain to Julia how ordinary it was when it happened. "I went to The Break with Karen and Amy, and Mr. Drury caught us."

Julia said, "What did you want to go and do a dumb thing like that for?"

"For heaven's sake!" I shouted at her. "Doesn't anybody in this house have the slightest bit of human sympathy? I don't know why we did it, but it didn't seem so horrible then, and now it's like it's the end of the world. I feel like I've betrayed my whole family, and nobody will even say one kind thing to me. How do you think I felt, waiting all week for you to find out? How do you think it feels to always be the dumb one and the sloppy one and the bad one in the family? It feels terrible, that's how! And my own sister doesn't even care!"

Julia reached out. "I'm sorry, Cath. I do care." But I ducked away from her hand and ran into the hall and up the steps. My chest was pounding and I was crying these long sobs, "Uh, uh, uh." I slammed the door of my room shut and kicked off my shoes and pulled down my window shade. Then I got inside the covers with all my clothes on and hugged the pillow and cried onto my pillowcase till it was wet. After a while, I went to sleep.

Eight

Mom woke me up later that night. I was sweating under the covers in my clothes. "Come down and eat something," she said.

I changed into pajamas and went downstairs. I didn't want to face Dad, but right away he said, "I think you feel bad enough, Catherine. Let's just talk about it and try to get it off our chests." That was so kind that I stopped feeling scared of him.

Julia had gone to bed. We sat at the kitchen table. Mom and Dad ate ice cream while I had some of the spaghetti I'd made.

"The lesson I want you to learn," Dad said, "is not about breaking this rule or that rule. The important thing is," and he pointed the cheese shaker at me, "that you learn to think about the consequences of what you do. You can't just rush off and do things without thinking. That's what you have to learn, Cathy."

"I know it, Dad," I said.

"How do you suppose your mother feels now?" Dad asked. "Do you think she wants to tell all her friends, or Aunt Rose, 'Cathy got suspended'?"

"No," I said.

"I think, myself, the school went too far, suspending you for the first mistake. But that doesn't help your mother. She feels ashamed. Now that's a terrible thing to do to someone who cares for you the way she does."

"Oh, I know," I said.

"And I feel it too," Dad went on. "I wouldn't like people at the store to hear about this. I hope no one does."

"I'm ashamed too!" I told him. "I hope all my teachers don't have to find out about it. I wish I didn't ever have to go to that school office again." I realized I didn't even know the facts of my suspension. I hadn't read the letter. "What days am I suspended for?" I asked.

"Tomorrow and the day after," Mom said. "Dad and I have talked it over, what you should do with the time. It shouldn't be a vacation. We want you to do something useful."

"I want to, too," I said.

"We think you should work one day at home," Mom said, "and another day at the store, helping Dad paint it. He's wanted to do that for a long time, but it takes two people to finish the job in a day."

"That won't be so awful," I said.

"The point is not how awful," Mom said. "The point is to make something useful out of it."

"That's good," I said. "I really want to show you how bad I feel I'm glad I can help out." Finally I said what

I had wanted to say for a long time. "I'm sorry. I'm really sorry I got suspended."

"I'm sorry, too," said Dad. "And I'm sorry the school saw fit to do it like this. I don't agree with it. Seems like pretty strong punishment to me. After all," he smiled, "what you did wasn't exactly criminal."

"But, Bob," Mom said, "remember, the school is responsible for hundreds of children. If one child should get hurt or be in an accident when they cut a class, you know their parents could raise an awful fuss."

"That's so," Dad said. "They use suspension to show they mean business."

I suppose that's true. But I don't think it works. Getting suspended didn't change my mind about going to The Break. I still don't think it was such an awful thing to do. The only awful part was getting caught.

I cleaned house all the next day, and I enjoyed it. I went from one downstairs room to the next, dusting and polishing the furniture and vacuuming and even washing windows. I waxed the kitchen floor. Then I carried the vacuum upstairs and did the bedrooms. Last of all, I scrubbed the bathroom. The house was shining when I was done. It smelled good and it looked peaceful. I could see how a person might enjoy doing housework. But I kept wondering how I would feel if this was someone else's house I was cleaning.

When I had finished, I called Karen. She wasn't home. The maid said she'd gone to the city with her mother. That's how crazy suspension is. If your parents are like Karen's, being suspended could just be like a holiday from school. I bet that if Karen's mother told her friends about it, she acted like Karen did something sort of silly or cute.

On the other hand, I was sorry for Amy. When I called her house, she said, "I can't talk. I have a lot of work to finish."

"I cleaned house all day," I said.

Amy said, " I have to work at home every afternoon for the next two weeks. I can't even go out of the house, except to school."

"Were your parents mad?" I asked.

"Yeah," said Amy. She didn't say any more. I can just imagine how mad her parents were. They wouldn't be reasonable like my parents. They get mad at Amy for the slightest thing. They're always "grounding" her. That means she has to stay home and not go out anywhere, for punishment.

"Come over after school when we go back and keep me company while I work," Amy said. "My mother won't be home. She's taking tennis lessons every day for the next two weeks."

"OK, see you the day after tomorrow," I said.

"See you," Amy said. She sounded sad.

I hope that if I am a parent when I grow up, I will remember how kids feel about things and not be mean to my own children. But then, I guess kids can be pretty tough. Look at Amy. She doesn't let her parents get her down. She has her own opinions and she's interested in her own things. Amy's parents made her take flute lessons from second grade on because they thought that was cultural. But Amy got much better than they ever expected. She is a really terrific flute player. I think she will be famous someday. She practices all the time. I wonder if she would have worked so hard at her flute if her parents had always been nice to her. I suppose so, but you never know.

The phone rang.

"Hi, Cath." It was Julia.

"Oh, hi, Julia," I said. I hadn't talked to her since I yelled at her yesterday. It may seem funny to be embarrassed to talk to your own sister, but I was.

"I just want to say I'm sorry about yesterday," Julia said. "I have a few minutes before I go back to the yearbook. I wanted to find out how you are, and tell you I'm sorry."

"Well, thanks, that's OK," I said. It wasn't really OK, though.

"No, it isn't," Julia said. "Sometimes I just don't think, you know? I don't know why I shoot my mouth off so fast. I didn't mean to sound superior or something. The thing is," she paused, "I'm really ashamed about what I said because I've been to The Break a couple of times. When I first went to high school. We just never got caught, that's all. I never told Mom and Dad, until last night, when you were upstairs."

"What did they say?" I asked. I was really surprised.

"They said they were glad I told them. They said it helped them to understand what you did. Then they said bygones should be bygones, but that I should tell you and say I'm sorry. Also they said I shouldn't get suspended now, when I am going to be class valedictorian, and please to be careful!"

"Thanks for telling them," I said.

"Yeah, well, I'm sorry I was so dumb yesterday. I hope you're not having a bad day?"

I told her I wasn't. "Actually it's sort of fun, being alone in the house. I cleaned. I vacuumed your room, but I didn't touch your desk."

"Thanks, Cath. That's nice. Listen, I have to go. See you at dinner, OK?"

"Yeah. Julia—"

"What?"

"You know, thanks for calling."

It was time for the mail to come. I went out to look for it. It was wonderful to look at the mailbox without worrying what would be in it. It was like getting well from flu and noticing how good it feels not to be sick. Usually, you're healthy without thinking about it.

I was hoping for a letter for Julia from one of the colleges she applied to. I can't believe they won't all accept her with a scholarship. But Julia says no. She says things are so tight that most colleges don't even give full scholarships any more. Without one, Julia just can't go away to school. We don't have enough money.

There was nothing for Julia. But the *Reader's Digest* came, so I took a break and sat down to read with a glass of ginger ale. I love the stories about "My Most Unforgettable Character." Some of those people are so funny or so nice. I always wish that somebody might think I was interesting enough to write about someday. I also like the *Reader's Digest* articles about people dying from some horrible disease. Either they die very bravely or else a miracle happens and they get well. I cry a lot when I read those stories, but it's kind of pleasant crying. The other articles I always read are called things like "How to Add Spice to Your Love-making." I think making love plain must be very interesting as it is, but I like those articles. Sometimes they help you figure out the things people actually do.

While I was reading, Mom came home.

"You're early!" I said.

"Yes, thank goodness," Mom said. "This has been a long week, but today was short *and* sweet. What a nice family the Estys are!"

"Who are they?"

"Well, they're people I heard about from Mrs. Saltera, one of the houseworkers I ride the bus with. Mrs. Saltera couldn't take on another job, so she suggested me. I'm so grateful to her. She's another one who wants to start up the houseworkers' group."

Suddenly, Mom stopped. "Cathy! The house looks beautiful. What a good job you've done! If this is what happens when you get suspended, maybe you ought to go out and cut class again tomorrow."

I knew she was feeling good. Mom doesn't often make that kind of joke. She usually says, "That isn't something to joke about."

"That isn't something to joke about, Mom," I said. I jumped up and hugged her.

Mom laughed and pulled me over to the couch. "It's so nice to come home from cleaning someone else's house and find my own so beautiful."

"Tell me about the Estys."

"First of all," Mom began, "they have this beautiful little baby, just the cutest thing you ever saw, only three weeks old—you wouldn't believe her little hands, how tiny they are!"

"What's her name?"

"Jenny."

Jenny happens to be one of my very favorite names, that I would consider naming my own child if I had one.

"The Estys are such a nice young couple," Mom went on. "Mr. Esty's a writer—I saw his name on the cover of a magazine on their coffee table. And Mrs. Esty doesn't look a day over twenty-five to me, but it turns out she's a psychologist over at Eastern State Hospital. She works with brain-damaged children and sometimes with elderly patients, too."

"How's she going to do that if she has this baby?"

"Between the two of them, they have it all worked out. Right now, Mrs. Esty is home on maternity leave. After about five weeks she's going to go back to work part-time in the afternoons, and Mr. Esty will take care of the baby while she's gone. He works at home anyway. You should see his study, Catherine. He has a desk the whole length of the room, covered with papers, and bookshelves from the floor to the ceiling, and books piled up on the floor besides. He says he has to clean his room himself because he's the only person who can tell what's trash and what's important."

"He sounds nice."

"He *is* nice. They both are. And that baby, what a little doll she is. I can't wait for you to see her."

"Why would *I* get to see her?"

"Listen, Cathy," Mom said, "this is the best part.

They asked me did I know anyone who could baby-sit for them, just now and then, like on weekends. They want somebody reliable and pleasant, they said. Mrs. Esty said, 'Mrs. Myers'—"

"They call you Mrs. Myers?"

"Yes, and I have to tell you I like it, no matter what I said before. A person gets sick of being called Clara by people who don't give two cents for her and only care about a clean house. Anyway, she said they want some-body who's nice and affectionate, that the baby could get to know and feel good with. And I said, 'That sounds like my Catherine.' "

"*Me?* Mom, I never even went *near* a baby! The only time I ever held one in my life was that boy Lisa Rommel's sister brought to Lisa's party, and he spit up all over me and cried the whole time I held him. Why didn't you say Julia?"

"Now, hon, you know Julia's busy with her last year, and the yearbook, and the check-out job. She can't take on any more than that. But the main reason I sug-gested you is that you are a nice person, and you're reliable and I think the baby would like you, and the Estys would like you, too. And you would like them."

"What if I can't do it right?"

"Don't be silly, Catherine. You'll do it right. It's pretty hard to ruin a baby."

"I don't even know how to change a diaper!" I said.

"Most people don't, until they have to. Then they learn. You'll learn. There's nothing mysterious about it."

"What if I dropped the baby?"

"You won't," said Mom firmly.

"But what—"

"You have more questions!" Mom said.

"What if the Estys don't even like me when they meet me? Did you tell them how old I am?"

"They said that was fine. Catherine, they're not hiring you to be the baby's *mother*. They just want somebody reliable to sit for them now and then, that's all."

Nobody knows better than me that I am not always a reliable person. It may sound funny, but I also know I *can* do things right if I want to enough. And I suddenly wanted very badly to take care of that little baby I didn't even know. I could just tell I would be good for her.

"I think I'd probably like to try it," I told Mom.

"Good," she said. "Now don't start worrying and getting scared about it. The Estys won't leave you alone with the baby until they know you can handle her. And remember, there's almost always someone home here. You're no further than a phone call from help."

"When will I meet them?" I asked. "Do they know I got suspended?"

"Of course not," Mom said. "That's nobody's business but our family's, and it's finished. I'm going to call Mrs. Esty and tell her you said yes," Mom went on. "Then I'll take you over there a week from Saturday. I'm going to clean up for them then because they have relatives coming."

This was Thursday. I had a week and a half to think about baby-sitting and about meeting the Estys.

Maybe they think I will be one of those high-school girls with a cute nose and a cheerleader sweater. Maybe they think I am extra nice because they know Mom. Maybe they think I am bright like Julia. I'm sure Mom's told them about Julia.

I hope they will like me.

Nine

The next day, Dad and I left extra early to paint the store. In a way, it seemed more like an adventure than a punishment. We brought sandwiches from home in a paper bag. Dad started coffee in the store's coffee maker. I could take a soda from the cooler any time I wanted. Dad had on an old pair of corduroy pants and a sweatshirt, and he looked almost as though he was on vacation. He never gets much of a real vacation, except Sundays at home and a week in the summer when we go to New Jersey, to the beach. It seemed like a vacation to me to be away from school on a Friday. It was hard to remember that I ought to be feeling guilty.

Dad put up the CLOSED sign on the front door. Then he put a pile of morning papers out on the sidewalk. "This way anyone who comes around to get a paper won't be disappointed," he said. "They can just throw down their money and take one."

First we cleared the walls. We took down posters

of people having beach picnics with sodas or splashing in mountain brooks with giant packs of cigarettes over their heads. We took down the old soda fountain menu and Dad threw it away. Most of the things on it were crossed out anyway. Dad stopped making sandwiches last year when the price of bread and lunch meat went too high. We covered all the counters and the magazine racks and the greeting card stands with dropcloths. Then we opened the first gallon of white paint.

"It's white all right," said Dad. "I'll say that for it. Now, how about you take one side and I'll do the ceiling?"

We each had a roller tray and a roller. You push the roller through the paint and then you roll it along the wall, first sideways and then up and down. If you put too much paint on, the roller just skids over the wall without really painting it. But when you begin to get the right system you can spread the paint on nice and smooth.

I moved right along, trying not to miss a single little place. The front door rattled. Someone was looking in the glass.

"Somebody's trying to get in," I said.

"I expect we'll get a lot of that," Dad said. "People just can't believe a CLOSED sign when they depend on you to be open. We'll have to ignore them while we're painting back here. When we get up front, I'll let people in if they knock."

I rolled a stripe of white paint right down to the baseboard. "I can't believe this wall was white before," I said. "It looks like dark gray next to the new paint."

"Been a long time since that was painted," said Dad. "Ten years, maybe. Your mother did it."

The paint smell got in my nose and throat. It wasn't horrible—this was latex paint—but it was strong and chalky. Pretty soon I had dripped enough paint on my hands and shirt to stop worrying about it. Now I was really going: fill, smooth off, roll on. The paint made a little splattering sound as it covered the wall. Dad stood on a counter near the back of the store. A fine spray of paint floated down from his arm. There were paint drips on his bald spot.

You can think about anything while you're painting along. My thoughts jumped from Dad's bald spot to Mom's work to George Waldman. I wish George didn't always have to show off and act so tough. I wonder if it's harder to be a boy. I would hate to have to fight and act strong all the time just to please other boys. Still, not all boys act like that. Look at Chris.

Suddenly I asked Dad, "Did you ever wish you had a boy?"

Dad pushed his roller tray up toward me with his foot. He pulled a paper towel out of his pants pocket and wiped his face. Then he set his roller down in the tray.

"Well, Catherine," he said, "I suppose there isn't a person alive who doesn't wonder what it would be like to have a child like them, the same sex. A woman with sons must wonder what daughters are like. Maybe you feel close in a special way to someone who is what you are—I think your mother feels that way about you girls. But I'll tell you the truth, you've always seemed pretty special to me, you and Julia. A man couldn't wish for better."

He smiled at me and picked up his roller and began to fill it with paint.

I rolled mine around and around in the tray and made a new stripe down the next part of the wall. It was strange to talk to Dad this way. We never usually talk much about our private ideas. It made me shy, but I wanted to keep on. I wanted to tell Dad that I could see why Julia makes him happy, but what about me?

"What about me?" I asked.

"What *about* you?"

"You know. That I'm not like Julia."

"You're not supposed to be like Julia."

"But don't you wish I was, sometimes? Julia never got suspended. Don't you wish I didn't?"

"Of course!" Dad said quickly. "Do you think I like it? Do you think your mother likes it? What do you want to ask me that for?"

"Because, see, Julia doesn't get into trouble, and I do, so I can't see why I make you happy."

"You *could* make me happier, it's true, said Dad. "I would be happier if you didn't get yourself suspended. I would be happier if you remembered to take out the garbage, and if you talked nicer to your Aunt Rose, and if you never yelled at your sister. Is that enough for you?" He sounded cross.

I turned away and rolled, very carefully, up to where the wall and ceiling met. For a while we just painted, not talking. I was thinking. I suppose Dad was, too.

"I got in trouble once, when I was about your age,"

67

Dad said all of a sudden. I looked at him, but he was staring hard at the ceiling while he painted around a pipe.

"What kind of trouble?" I asked.

"A friend of mine and I, we each took a bicycle light out of a display at the hardware store. We thought no one was looking, but the owner's wife happened to come in from the back of the store and she caught us."

"What happened?"

"First they wanted to take us to the police, but then they decided just to call our parents instead. My dad walked out of his drugstore and right across the street into that hardware store and whapped me. Then he took me home and told my mother. Mother was all wrought up. In the end, I had to pay the hardware-store man, that was all. But the shame to my parents was terrible."

"Did you ever tell Mom about it?" I asked.

"Why, no, I guess I never had the occasion to tell her," Dad said.

Imagine Dad telling me something Mom doesn't even know!

I had to think about that some. It was a surprise to me, because Dad is always so honest and good. I bet he took the bicycle light on the spur of the moment, without really meaning to.

Dad said, "I sometimes think you and I are pretty much alike. Me having an older brother to keep up with, and you Julia."

"Was Uncle Dick smart?"

Uncle Dick sells cars in Boston, Massachusetts. He has three little boys and a wife called Aunt Mary. They send us a three-pound fruitcake every Christmas, but we hardly ever see them.

"I don't know about smart. He seemed to know just what he wanted, though. He had a year of college before he took that summer job with the Ford dealer. And from then on it was smooth sailing. His own business by the time he was twenty-five, a well-to-do man by thirty."

I picked up a dropcloth that fell to the floor.

"Did you like Uncle Dick a lot?"

"Not a whole lot," Dad said. "It wasn't the same as you and your sister. There were eight years between us and that's pretty much of a difference when you're young. I liked to be with him, of course, but it wasn't the same as having a brother close to my own age."

"Did people expect you to be like him?"

"Oh, I don't know about that. I don't know if people expected it. It was mostly me, I guess. I wanted to go places and be a success like Dick. Not that I envy him his line of work. Not for a minute. Sometimes, though, I wish I could have provided for your mother and you girls the way Dick does for his family."

Dad poured some paint from the gallon can into his roller tray. "Looks like we're going to need more of this pretty soon."

I think Dad wanted to stop talking about Uncle Dick. I'm glad he told me, though. It makes me feel closer to Dad to know about his feelings. And to know that he once got into trouble. That was interesting. Maybe someday I can tell my own child about how I got suspended, and make her feel good!

I've met Uncle Dick a couple of times. I don't remember much about him except that he's big and he talks very loud, and once he called me "Baby Doll" and I didn't like it.

"One thing for sure," I said. "I'm glad you're my father, not Uncle Dick."

"Thanks for the compliment," Dad said, smiling at me. "Now let's see if we can find a good stopping place and knock off for some lunch. You hungry?"

I hadn't thought about it, but I was. "Just let me finish up this last section and the whole side will be done," I said.

"Go right ahead, don't let me stop you," said Dad. "You've got a good-looking wall there."

By now we had put on so much paint that the whole store was brighter. I concentrated on filling in the last section of my side, right up to the ceiling line. It was like filling in a giant coloring-book picture of a wall. One last sideways roll, one last up-and-down roll. A little smoothing-over roll.

"Done!" I said. "Want me to set out the lunch?"

"Get yourself a soft drink and pour me a mug of that coffee," Dad said. "I'll be right with you soon as I set these rollers in water."

"Oh, I forgot. Mine's in my roller tray. Sorry."

"That's OK. We just want to keep them soft over our lunch break."

I took a diet cola out of the cooler. Mom always

makes us drink diet soda so we won't ruin our teeth with sugar. Sometimes I think that when I'm grown up I'll celebrate by drinking all the real tooth-decay soda I can hold. But I probably won't. It is disgusting to think of all that sugar sort of hanging onto your teeth.

I went back to clean up in Dad's little washroom. It's just big enough for a toilet and a washbasin. When I looked in the mirror, I was surprised. I had streaks of paint in my hair and on my face and neck. But most of it came off pretty easily with water.

When Dad had finished cleaning up, I had our lunch set out on the counter. We had egg salad sandwiches, lots of pickles, some carrot sticks, and an apple each. Coffee for Dad, soda for me. I was hungry! We sat on stools next to each other and ate nice and slow. It felt good to sit after squatting and stretching all morning long.

Someone banged on the front door. We looked up.

"That's Jim Dailey," Dad said. "Let's see what he wants."

He got up and unlocked the door, and Mr. Dailey stepped inside. "What's going on here, Bob?" he asked. "Looks like you got some nonunion labor there, ha, ha."

"Giving the place a spring cleaning," said Dad. "Can I offer you a cup of coffee?"

"No thanks, Bob, no thanks, I've gotta get on my way," said Mr. Dailey. "Besides, if I stay around here it looks like I might get pressed into work!"

"No, sir, I've got all the help I need in my girl here," Dad said. "Catherine, have you met Mr. Dailey proper before?"

71

I held out my hand, but then I pulled it back. "I'm pleased to meet you, Mr. Dailey," I said. "But I guess you don't want to shake my painty hand."

"Well, well, now, pleased to meet *you,* young lady," said Mr. Dailey. "Many's the time your father used to show me your picture when you were a little girl. I must say I didn't realize you were this age already."

My father was smiling at us. "Come on, Jim, a half cup won't hurt you."

"No, Bob, I can't. Have to be on my way. Sorry to barge in on you folks, but it seems like I can't be in this part of town without stopping in at Bob's. It's like a habit. When you planning to open up again?"

"I think we'll be back to normal tomorrow," Dad said, "with Catherine here to help me set things back."

"You're a lucky man," Mr. Dailey said. "I hope that other girl of yours—what's her name now? Oh, yes, Julia. I hope she's as fine a help to you as Catherine."

I started to explain how helpful Julia is, but Mr. Dailey was tipping his cap and looking at his watch and turning the front doorknob. "God bless you, honey," he said to me. "Take care, now, Bob," he said to Dad. "Don't tip over any paint cans, ha, ha!"

It seemed pretty quiet after Mr. Dailey left.

"He's nice," I said.

"A good man," said Dad. "That man, by himself, pays for the kids' lunches down at the day-care center. Buys peanut butter and crackers and juice in bulk at the A&P and stocks their cupboards once a month, and makes no noise about it. Only reason I know is, once in a while he gives them money for paper and crayons and paste and the teacher comes down here and chooses what she needs. She told me about the lunches."

"I never realized how many people come around," I said.

"Oh, yes," said Dad. "Of course, it isn't the way it used to be. The volume of business is way down. Still and all, people keep dropping in to talk over the weather or the news and drink a cup of coffee. It's a sociable business, Catherine. People like the chance to relax and exchange a few words while they pick up their papers."

"It's like having friends drop in all the time," I said.

"Well, yes, you could say that," said Dad. "I like to make people feel welcome and it does something for me to know that folks appreciate it."

I didn't realize this before. My mother and dad have friends that they have over for bridge or go to the movies with. But Dad has friends from all over town because of the store. All afternoon, while we painted the other wall and cleaned the shelves and painted them and rearranged supplies in the showcases, people kept stopping by. I must have been introduced to at least eight people. Not a single one of them asked if I was as smart as Julia. They all said how lucky Dad was to have me.

At the end of the day we washed up and took turns changing out of our paint clothes. Dad took the

CLOSED sign off the door. Before he locked up, we stood in the doorway and looked at the store. It was really bright and cheerful.

"That's a good day's work, Catherine," Dad said. "I've got a hard-working daughter." He didn't mention the suspension.

"Thanks," I said. "Wait till Mom and Julia see what we did! Wait till your customers walk in tomorrow."

We walked home carrying our rollers and roller trays and paint clothes. The air was soft with that sweet smell of new leaves and onion grass. It was almost spring.

I felt free and almost easy. The suspension was over and I had worked hard to help my folks. There was just one thing still nagging at me. I had never told Karen and Amy about Mom's work.

Ten

When you've been absent from school, you're supposed to bring an excuse from home to the office. It seemed as though I ought to have a note this time, too: "Please excuse Cathy for being absent. She was suspended." But no one expected a note. In a way, the whole suspension thing didn't seem so well organized. Nobody really talked to us when it happened, except Mrs. Vogel. And there was nobody to talk to after it was over.

I walked in the school door and went past the office to my locker, same as always. School was the same, too. A hall aide was standing next to my locker holding a baseball glove and arguing with two boys who had been playing catch with it in the hall. People were banging locker doors and calling to their friends. I looked up and saw Karen.

"Hi! How did you like suspension?" I asked.

"Listen, guess what?" she said. "I *am* going to go to boarding school next year."

"Really?"

"Yeah. I went with Mom on Friday to talk to people from this one school in Connecticut. It sounds neat. There's only sixty kids in the whole school, and you can have your own horse and keep him in a barn there."

"Do you think you'll go there?" I asked. I hadn't expected Karen to decide so fast. I was surprised. In a way, my feelings were hurt.

"I don't know. Mom wants me to look at some other schools. But I'm definitely going to go to boarding school somewhere. Mom says Camden High isn't the greatest if you want to get into a good college."

"Well, it's good enough for Julia," I said, feeling scared that maybe it wasn't. Julia still hadn't heard from any college.

"Oh, sure, I didn't mean Julia," Karen said quickly. "But for someone like me."

Or me, I thought. All I have on my record is ordinary grades. And a suspension.

The bell rang and we went on to Mrs. Inman's class. So many things were happening. Suspension was over. School was going to be over soon—only eight weeks to go. Julia would be graduating. Next year I'd be in ninth grade, and Karen would be away at boarding school. A lot of changes. I wasn't sure I was ready.

Mrs. Inman smiled at us. "Hello, girls. I see on the teachers' announcements that you were suspended last week. How in the world did that happen?"

"They cancelled our gym class and we went to The Break," I said.

"That doesn't seem so terrible," said Mrs. Inman. "But there *is* a rule and if you get caught, that's it."

"It's funny, though," I said. "Nobody even talked with us about it. They just sent letters to our parents."

"How did you spend the time?" Mrs. Inman asked.

"Cleaned my house and helped my father paint his store," I said. "It wasn't bad."

"I went for an interview at a boarding school," Karen said.

"Oh? How was it?"

"I liked it," Karen said. "Anyway, I'm going to go away to some school next year."

"In a way I'm sorry to hear that," Mrs. Inman said. "I always think one of the good things about Camden is the mixture of people who go to it. I would hate to see the kids from wealthy families leave."

Mrs. Inman is so frank! I don't know anyone else who would just come out and talk about things like money and people's differences. I agree with her, but it's hard for me to say it. Especially because in some ways I know I'm just jealous.

"Now, Cathy, how are you coming with the reading-tutors project?" Mrs. Inman asked me.

"Well, see, I was waiting for you to help me get in touch with Allen School, and then I was away being suspended," I said. "So I haven't really got started yet." I wished I had. Why didn't I think about it last week?

"Come on, Cathy," she said, sort of disapprovingly, "you don't need *me* to put you in touch with Allen

School, do you really? What's the name of the teacher there your mother worked with?"

"Mrs. Pflaum."

"Well, the way to begin, I should think, is just to call up Mrs. Pflaum and ask her."

I was surprised. I hadn't expected to do the arranging myself. I thought that Mrs. Inman would call them first and explain the project. The thing is, I am sort of embarrassed about making phone calls. I hate trying to explain something complicated over the phone. I always think I won't be able to talk fast enough and the person will hang up on me. Or they won't understand me.

But Mrs. Inman seemed to expect me to go ahead. "Shall I do it after school?" I asked.

"Why don't you do it right now," Mrs. Inman said. "Just go down to the office and tell them I said to let you use the phone. Call the Allen School office and tell them you want to talk to Mrs. Pflaum. OK?"

"OK."

"Go ahead, then. You'll miss some of our discussion on housing, but you can catch up from Karen later on."

Kids in the room were standing around talking. "Get settled, will you?" Mrs. Inman asked them. She wrote me a pass to go to the office.

I had to show the pass to one school aide who was wearing a checked pants suit and standing with her arms folded in the middle of Hall B. She just grunted and let me pass.

Mrs. Vogel looked up when I came in the office. "Back at school, are you?"

"Yes," I said. "Can I use the phone? I have to make a call to Allen School. It's for a project with Mrs. Inman."

"Sure, over there," she said.

It's funny how things that worry you a lot don't mean anything to other people. I suppose Mrs. Vogel sees so many kids get suspended that she doesn't think much about it. All morning I had felt as though I should apologize to people. But I began to feel more ordinary after I saw how Mrs. Vogel acted.

It was hard to do the phone call right. I couldn't even figure out how to get a dial tone. Mrs. Vogel explained I had to dial nine first. Then when I got through to the Allen School office, I got cut off after I said a few words. So I had to dial again. I had the feeling that everybody in the school office was listening to me. Finally, I got through to Mrs. Pflaum. It was easy with her. When I mentioned my mother she got very friendly, and when I explained my idea about volunteer tutors she sounded pleased and interested. I made a date to ride my bike to Allen School and talk with her at the end of the day.

At lunch in the cafeteria, Amy said, "All the eighth-graders in orchestra are going to Camden High today to practice with the high-school orchestra for graduation."

"Will you be in orchestra next year?" Chris asked.

"Oh, sure," Amy said. "I can't wait. Mr. Howard is a terrific conductor and I love the music they do. It's good music, not things like 'Jingle Bells Variations' that we have to play in this school."

Chris said, "I can't wait to get into the photography lab. It's going to be neat."

"I'm going over to work on the yearbook this week," I said.

"You are? How come?" Chris asked.

"Well, Julia needed some extra help and she said I could," I told him.

"You're lucky, Cathy," Amy said. "You'll get to know the yearbook people and you might get on the staff next year."

I hadn't thought of that.

Karen said, "You guys are going to have fun, being together in high school. I'll miss you."

I hadn't thought of that, either. I suppose, in a way, Karen will be jealous of *us*.

"My parents thought maybe the high school wouldn't let me in," Amy said, "because I got suspended. Can you imagine?"

"Mrs. Vogel hardly said anything to me when I went to the office this morning," I told her.

"You had to go to the *office*?" Amy asked. She sounded panicked.

"Just to make a phone call." I explained about the reading-tutors project.

Amy said she didn't think she would want to work with little kids that way. But Chris thought it sounded interesting.

"It's awfully late to start, though," he said. "You ought to begin something like that in the fall."

Mrs. Pflaum said the same thing, later that afternoon.

"But that's OK," she said. "We always work a long

way ahead. You and I could do some background research and planning now, and get a good head start on
next year."

"But I'll be in high school next year!" I said.

Mrs. Pflaum laughed. "That's not the end of the
world, I should think."

"The thing is, I want to get credit for a project with
Mrs. Inman *this* year," I explained, sort of embarrassed.

Mrs. Pflaum has a way of making things seem easy.
I bet she's a good first-grade teacher. She said, "I'm sure
Mrs. Inman would be glad to give you credit for doing
some background reading and making up a plan for
using student volunteers. Then she could use the plan
with her students next year, or you might want to go on
with it yourself in high school."

Mrs. Pflaum took me around her room. She showed
me books and games and posters and signs she uses to
help her kids learn to read. Her room is the same one I
had in third grade. The chairs and tables are still painted
light green, but everything else is different. Still, I
could remember just where George Waldman used to
sit and make paper airplanes and sail them at you when
the teacher left the room. Mrs. Pflaum had a few of
those readers about Dick and Jane and Spot, but most of
her books were the other kind—real stories, with interesting pictures. I read a funny one called *Frog and Toad*.

"How could I start to learn what books kids like?"
I asked.

"The first thing you might do is just go to the library
and read a lot yourself," Mrs. Pflaum said. "Ask the
librarian for some easy-to-read books, and ask her what

81

books the six- and seven-year-olds like best. That way you'll get a good introduction to young children's reading."

Then she gave me a couple of magazines with writing by teachers and by kids, and she gave me an article she had read in graduate school, about how older kids can help teach younger ones. I didn't know people studied things like that.

"Do you think I could come and visit your class someday?" I asked. "I'd love to see what it's like when the kids are here. I want to meet Bobby Arvin, too." I told her how my mother talked about him.

"Oh, Bobby talks about your mom, too," Mrs. Pflaum said. "He really misses her. What kind of work did your mother find, Catherine?"

"Just housework," I said. It was bad enough to have to tell Mrs. Pflaum. It was going to be much worse to tell my friends.

Eleven

I wasn't sure what I was afraid of. I'm not dumb enough to think that Karen or Amy would stop liking me if I told them Mom was a cleaning lady. I guess I worried that they might feel different about Mom, and then about me, because of it. They're used to treating people who do their housework in a special way—they either boss them around or ignore them. It's as though Amy's mother's cleaning lady and the maid at Karen's house aren't real people. My mother *is* a real person. I want people to understand that.

After school the next day, Karen and I rode Amy's bus so we could talk while she worked at home. It's Chris's bus, too. I like it. It's much quieter than my bus and George Waldman isn't on it. So I don't have to keep protecting myself.

Karen and Amy and I squeezed into a seat in front of Chris and Johnny Stone. They were kidding us about being suspended.

"I'm surprised they even let you on the bus," Johnny said.

"Yeah, they ought to keep innocent people like us away from you," said Chris. "The problem is, you don't *look* like criminals. They should make you wear big red S's, the way that lady in *The Scarlet Letter* wore an *A*, to warn people off."

"Oh, stop it," I said. "Don't be dumb."

But actually it was fun to kid around like that after days of feeling guilty. Things were getting back to normal. I just had to tell Karen and Amy about Mom's work and get that over with. Then I'd feel great.

"Hey, here's my stop," Chris said suddenly. "Hey, stop!" he called to the bus driver. "Let me off!"

He grabbed his books and his jacket and ran up to the front of the bus. The driver stopped. We laughed and waved at him out the window.

Amy's stop was next. We said so long to John and got off.

I don't like Amy's house too much. It's exactly like all the other houses on her street, except for the color. Amy's is pale blue. The houses have perfect green lawns and curving driveways and porches with four skinny pillars and a lamp hanging down on a big black chain. I always worry that the lamp will fall on my head while I'm waiting to get in.

There was a note from Amy's mother on the kitchen table.

"Oh, boy," Amy said. "Look at this." The note said:

1. Sort dry laundry and put away.
2. Clean refrige (don't forget freezer).
3. Fix dinner (menu on bulletin board).
4. Don't let girls out of yard.
I will be home by seven and expect to find things done by then and your homework started. Mother.
P.S. Don't waste time on telephone.

"Maybe we should go," Karen said. "We'll be in the way."

"No you won't," said Amy. "Stick around. It won't be so bad if I have company."

"Would your mother mind?" I asked.

"She won't know," Amy said. She put ginger ale and glasses on the table and found some cookies.

I hoped Amy's mother wouldn't come home early. I'm sort of scared of her. I would hate to get a note like that from my mother. My mother always begins her notes, "Dear Catherine." At the end she writes, "Love, Mom."

"My mom's been acting really bitchy lately," Karen said. I knew she was trying to make Amy feel better about the note. The same way she'd try to make me feel better when I told her about Mom. But that's part of the problem. I don't want Amy and Karen to try to be sympathetic about Mom. You have to love someone to sympathize in an understanding way. The other kind of sympathy is almost like an insult.

Karen went on, "Mom has this new deadline schedule and one of her assistants left and the advertising went down this quarter. And the publisher says the magazine's lagging behind the times. That's what bothers Mom. She can't figure out what the magazine ought to say, whether it should tell more about careers or about beauty and cooking or whatever. She wants to do controversial articles about things like Zero Population Growth, but then some readers get mad. Mom gets so nervous when she plans issues for next year."

"One kind of article she should have," Amy said, "is how to go out and get some work besides being a mother and playing tennis and bridge and shopping." She was sorting the girls' underwear into piles on the table. There was a lot of it.

"It isn't that easy to get a job!" I blurted out. *"That's* what magazines should tell you. Everybody tells women, 'Go back to work, go back to work,' and then when people go out to look for it, there isn't any decent work. It's not fair!" I was angry that Karen and Amy didn't know about things like unemployment and layoffs and real job hunting. "You know what happened to my mom?" I demanded. "You don't even know how tough things are. My mom tried to go back to work and she couldn't find any work except house cleaning." I made myself look right at them. "So Mom's a cleaning lady. Right now. She's probably out somewhere near your house this very minute, Karen, scrubbing floors."

Well, I'd said it.

Amy put a little pair of flowered underpants on a pile. "That's terrible!" she said. "I mean, she ought to get some work that's more, you know, interesting. Why didn't she look in the help-wanted ads and stuff like that?"

"She *did*!" I said. How could Amy be so dumb? "She looked everywhere. They said she didn't have enough experience for anything but factory work or house-cleaning."

"I don't see what's so bad about it," Karen said. She *was* trying to make me feel good, the way I knew she would. "Mom says Dorca really has it made, working at her own speed in a nice house and getting her meals free and everything." Dorca is their maid.

I yelled, "Karen! How can you say that? How would you like to work in somebody else's house and they never paid any attention to you because you're just the maid? How would *you* like to scrub other people's floors and clean their bathrooms and not even get decent pay for it? And have to act grateful when people give you their old castoffs?"

"Well, I wouldn't," Karen said calmly. "But some-body has to. That's the way it is."

What I thought is that it's a lot easier to talk about "the way it is" if you're rich.

"It does seem sort of unfair," Amy said. She had fin-ished sorting the laundry and now she was pulling pack-ages out of the refrigerator. She made a face.

"Look at this disgusting roast beef!"

It was a beautiful pink roast with greenish mould on the brown crust. I love roast beef. We hardly ever have it.

"Couldn't you just cut off the edge?" I asked. "The rest of it looks OK."

"It's too gross," Amy said. "I wouldn't want to touch it, much less eat it." She threw the whole package into the garbage can. I couldn't help thinking that roast beef costs more a pound than Mom makes in an hour.

Amy said, "It's too bad about your mom, Cathy. I mean, it's too bad she couldn't find the kind of work she wanted. But you want to know something? I wouldn't mind *what* kind of work my mother did, honestly, if only she would do something besides buy clothes and get her hair done and tell me how to behave." She threw away two spoiled oranges and a brown head of lettuce.

It's true. I know Amy wishes her mother had something to do. I mean, she has these three little girls besides Amy, but she doesn't even seem to care about them. Amy doesn't like to have to take care of her sisters all the time, but at least she loves them. She's the one who usually kisses them goodnight.

You wouldn't believe how many kinds of sauces and mustard and pickles were in Amy's refrigerator. Amy threw half of them out. "They smell funny," she said. She kept making faces and Karen kept laughing at her.

I guess my news about Mom didn't really bother them too much. Or they didn't want to think about it. I was relieved, but in a way I was sorry, too. Someday I'd like to have friends who truly understand me. But I suppose nobody really understands another person's life. That's one thing about a sister. You share an awful lot.

When Julia and I were little, we used to stay over at people's houses and come back and tell Mom: "At Cynthia's house they have color TV!" "Amy gets two dollars allowance every week." "Guess what? Mr.

Thompson took us to the Dairy Queen and we could order whatever we wanted!"

I wonder if we made Mom feel bad. She'd listen to us and then she'd say, "It's good for you to see how other folks live. Just don't forget, life isn't all smooth sailing for anyone. And if you start feeling sorry for yourself, remember all the poor people in this world who don't even have enough to eat or a decent place to live or a family to care for them. We should count our blessings."

When I was younger—I guess up till now—I used to think I could count my blessings easier if I only had a new winter coat besides or a better bike. But now I don't know. There are different kinds of blessings. I can see that Mom is one of mine.

The doorbell rang, and rang, and rang, and rang. Amy's little sisters were home from school. It was time to go.

"Come on home with me, Karen," I said. "Eat dinner at my house and Dad will take you home after."

"Can I?" said Karen. "That would be nice. It's been a long time since I was over."

The girls were climbing on chairs and grabbing things off the table. "Hold it, hold it!" Amy yelled. "I'll fix you something good if you take it easy. How about toasted cheese?" Amy is so nice to her sisters. They really look up to her.

She was buttering bread and listening to news of the fifth-grade softball tournament when we left.

"So long," we said. "Hope you get it all done," I added.

"Don't waste time on telephone!" Karen ordered.

Amy laughed.

Karen and I matched our steps down the driveway. The sun was so hot I took off my sweater. Spring was really here.

Twelve

George Waldman died.

I can't believe it. I just can't believe it.

I was at Chris's doing biology homework and watching his mother polish her newest piece of jewelry, a wide gold bracelet that curves like a wave around your wrist. Chris and I went upstairs for apples and the phone rang. It was Amy. I could hear even though Chris got the phone.

"Did you hear about George Waldman?" Amy asked.

"No, what?" Chris said.

"He died."

"Died!" Chris shouted. "Are you kidding, Amy?"

"Ask her what happened," I said. "Ask her!"

"George and Kenny Brown were fooling around with his mother's gun that she keeps in her bedroom," Amy said. "George showed Kenny how you load it, and then he put it on a table and then George and Kenny both grabbed for it, and somehow the gun went off." Her voice sounded like a recording. "George was bending over the table and the bullet hit him in the head. Kenny tried to stop the bleeding and then he ran next door and got the neighbor and when they came back George was dead. They called the ambulance, but when the driver came he said George must have died instantly."

"Oh, my God," I said.

"What happened to Kenny?" Chris asked.

"They took him to the police station, but they didn't keep him. I guess they believed his story. When George's mother came she said she knew George fooled around with her gun, even though he promised her he wouldn't."

I could see George Waldman in my head as clear as day throwing some kid's hat out the bus window. But I couldn't imagine him lying on the floor with blood coming out of him, dead.

"Oh, Chris, it's so awful!" I said.

"What's going to happen now?" Chris asked Amy.

"Mr. Gottsegen is at his house, and so is Mrs. Inman," Amy said. Her voice sounded sharp and scared. "His father is flying up from Florida."

I took the phone from Chris.

"Amy, I can't believe it," I said.

"I know," Amy said. "I can't either. Listen, Cathy, I have to go."

"OK, see you," I said, automatically, as though it were a regular phone call. "Amy—thanks for telling us," I added.

"Bye," she said.

"Oh, Chris," I said. "I just can't believe it." How could they have been so careless? If only George hadn't known about his mother's gun. "Just imagine how horrible Kenny must feel. It must be so awful to see your friend die. Oh, Chris!"

Then Chris did a kind thing. He came over and put his arms around me and stood there. He didn't squeeze me or anything. I felt so comforted, standing quietly that way.

After a while Chris said, "I guess we should tell my mother." So we went down to her workroom and Chris said, "Listen, Ma, Amy just called and said that a boy in our school, George Waldman, got shot with a gun. And he died."

"Oh, no!" said Chris's mother. She pushed her stool away from her workbench and jumped down. "Oh, Chris, that's terrible! How did it happen?"

Chris told her how Kenny and George were fooling around with the gun.

"Oh, that poor boy, watching his friend die," Chris's mother said. "What a terrible thing! People never should have guns around. Those accidents happen all the time. And it's such a waste!"

I tried to think about Kenny. I couldn't imagine how he felt. It was so scary just to think about George being dead. I didn't see how Kenny could bear to be with him when he was dying. He must feel so awful. How will he ever look at George's mother again?

"Where are his parents?" Chris's mother asked.

"His mother's a waitress at the coffee shop in the

mall," I said. "His father's in Florida. Amy said his father was coming up. Oh, Mrs. Rosen, I feel so terrible!"

"Did you know him well, Cathy?" she asked.

"Oh, yes, I've known him ever since Allen School," I told her. "He rides my school bus. Rode."

That's what dead means. You don't ride the school bus any more. You don't tease little kids and whisper at girls and snicker in the back of the human relations class. You're dead.

"I always hated him, Mrs. Rosen!" I said. "He was so mean all the time. And now I feel so awful!"

"Let me make you some tea," she said. "Chris, put the kettle on, will you?" She has a little hot plate in her workroom.

She set out cups and saucers and put a tea bag in each cup. "Want a cookie, Cathy? Chris?"

We said no.

Chris said, "You must really feel funny, Cathy. I don't know George Waldman half as well as you do. Did."

His mother had found a lemon and was cutting it into slices. She did it so neatly. "Lemon, Cathy?"

When she asked that, I started to cry. I put my head down on the workbench and let go, without even worrying what they would think of me. I cried so hard my chest hurt. I couldn't stop thinking about George Waldman with blood coming out of his head.

Chris and his mother talked quietly while I cried. Mrs. Rosen rubbed my shoulder. After a while, I went to their bathroom and washed my face and Mrs. Rosen drove me home. She said I'd probably want to be there when my mother came home so I could tell her.

"Where is she working today?" she asked.

"At the Estys," I said. It's easy to talk about Mom's work to Mrs. Rosen. I told Chris a while ago and he told her, and all she said to me was, "Now that your mother's working, Cathy, you know you're welcome to come over here any afternoon." She didn't make any big thing of it.

My house was very empty. I sat down on the couch and tried to believe what had happened. I didn't cry. I couldn't seem to believe it.

Then Julia came home.

"Oh, Cathy, I just heard about George Waldman!"

"I can't even believe it," I said.

"I don't see how we'll ever believe it," said Julia. "That poor Kenny Brown! I feel so sorry for him. I know his brother. What a terrible thing for their family!"

Mom came in looking shocked. "Oh, girls, I just heard. Isn't it awful? I don't know how I can help. Poor Mrs. Waldman, with her husband gone, and now this. That poor woman, she always tried so hard to do things right. She used to come to PTA meetings and sit through them and never say a word. She was a class mother at Allen School I don't know how many years. But she always kept to herself. I knew that boy of hers was a worry to her."

"I hated him, Mom!" I said. "And now I'm so sorry, really and truly, I'm so sorry! I'd do anything to make George Waldman be alive again."

"There's nothing anyone can do, Catherine," Mom said, "except to try to help Mrs. Waldman. I'm going to go over there when Dad comes home, hard as it will be, and ask if I can do something. Maybe she'll want someone just to sit with her. Maybe you could write a little note, since you've known George so long."

"Oh, Mom, what can I say?" I asked. "I don't know how to say anything."

"You'll have to say whatever you can that's kind, and true," Mom told me. "Letters will mean a lot to Mrs. Waldman. But she won't want to read a lot of sentimental lies."

Poor Mrs. Waldman. I bet she wanted good things for George the same as Mom and Dad want for us. Everybody must hope their children will be successful and happy. And now Mrs. Waldman's son was dead, with no more chances.

It was so unfair. People who die should be heroes, not just get shot in some dumb accident. I bet George was trying to show off to Kenny with his mother's gun. I bet he wished he was some kind of TV hotshot. That's probably why he got the gun out in the first place. I wonder what George Waldman used to think about. I wonder what he wanted to grow up and be. Now he won't ever be anything.

"I always treated him so mean!" I said.

"He treated you mean, Cathy," Julia said. "I used to see him on the bus. Don't you start feeling guilty."

"That's right," Mom said. "Nobody's guilty. It's just a sad thing those boys had to fool around with a gun. Mrs. Waldman should never have had a gun

96

around in the first place. Now that it's too late, you watch, we'll hear a lot about the danger of guns. Your father would never keep one for that very reason. It's just too risky."

Dad came home late. People had kept coming into the store to ask about George Waldman. Already rumors were starting. Dad said it looked as though Kenny would have to go through some kind of a hearing even though everyone was sure he was innocent. "It's a horrible situation," Dad said. "It makes a man feel grateful to have his family safe around him." He smiled in a sad, serious way, full of love for us.

In bed that night, I couldn't stop thinking about George Waldman on the bus. I wonder why he pestered me so much. I wonder how I could have helped him? I hope he had some good times in his life when he was a little boy and his dad was around. I wonder if he knew he was dying when he died. It must feel so horrible to have a bullet smash into your head!

How could I ever get so worried about my own little petty troubles?

Now George Waldman is dead.

Oh, I never want to die!

Thirteen

I didn't go to the funeral. Mom said I didn't have to, and I was glad. I did write Mrs. Waldman a note. I worked very hard to say only true things. I said I had known George almost all my life and that I was sorry he was dead. That it seemed like a terrible thing for somebody my age to die. And that I sent her my sympathy.

I didn't say how I really felt about George. But what I did say was true. I do feel sorry for his mother. Now she will be living alone. I hope she will find a way to make new things happen in her life.

Mrs. Inman talked about the accident in our human relations class. She even said that sometimes people fool with guns to make themselves seem stronger than they really feel. In a way, I thought it wasn't so polite to mention that. But I thought it was helpful to talk about accidents and gun control. And how shooting and killing is so ordinary on television that death doesn't seem like anything, until somebody you know dies. I think everyone felt better after we had talked. Even Jimmy Rizzo and Bernie Muller. They had been pallbearers at the funeral.

Mrs. Inman said that everybody is scared of dying and that it's natural for us to feel more scared when someone we know has died, especially somebody our own age.

"I think George was quite unhappy sometimes," she said, "and I think we ought to have been more ready to help him. I feel especially bad that he didn't get to carry out his project for this class. He was very serious about it. He wanted to do a report on restaurants— how customers treat the waitresses, and how waitresses treat cooks, and cooks treat dishwashers, and so on. It was an interesting, original project idea. And George wanted to do it because he thought his mother had a tough time being a waitress. He wanted to be a kind of reporter, investigating the restaurant."

"Did his mother know?" I asked.

"Yes," Mrs. Inman said, "but not until afterwards. I told her about the project after George had died. She was so pleased to know he had wanted to do that study. She felt it showed he cared a lot about her. And I think it did."

I felt as though I had to confess. "George Waldman made me awfully mad sometimes, Mrs. Inman. He always used to be mean to me."

I was sorry after I said it. You are not supposed to say bad things about dead people.

"She shouldn't speak evil of the dead, Mrs. Inman," Jimmy Rizzo said.

Karen said, "She's trying to tell the truth."

"Does anyone here know how Cathy feels?" Mrs. Inman asked.

Bernie Muller! He said, "Yeah, I do. Sometimes George would pick on me. Now he's dead and I was a pallbearer and all." He sort of ducked his head and looked up at Mrs. Inman. That was the most he had said all semester. I thought he was brave to say it.

Mrs. Inman said, "One thing about a friend is he's someone who likes you even though you have faults. I'm sure it was hard for you to be a pallbearer and face Mrs. Waldman, Bernie. You should feel proud to have done it."

Bernie said, "George was really funny sometimes, he could have been a comedian. He did these imitations— he used to break me up with an imitation of Mr. Gross."

"Yeah!" Jimmy Rizzo added. "He was really good. He could imitate anybody in this school. You should of seen him do Mrs. Vogel, 'Oh, I'm sorry, boys and girls, you'll all have to get late passes.' "

Bernie laughed. We all did. It was good to think of George in a funny way. That made a good memory. We were all feeling better when the bell rang.

But it was still hard to believe. Only last week, George Waldman sat in the back of this class, fooling around and snickering. Now he is buried in the ground. It doesn't seem possible that things could change so fast.

Some people at school took up a collection to give money to UNICEF in George's name. I think that was a good idea. I gave two dollars. And yesterday in assembly the orchestra dedicated a piece to George. Amy said afterward that some kids didn't want to because they didn't like George. How petty can you get?

It makes me see how petty I am sometimes. Worrying about how poor my family is, and things like that, when I should feel lucky that I *have* a family, all together.

Still, I can't help worrying about Julia. Yesterday, when I got home from school there was a letter for her from M.I.T. I kept hoping all afternoon, but when Julia came home and opened the letter, it said, "We are sorry to inform you that your application for admission to M.I.T. for the coming year is among those that have not been accepted. We hope you will understand that many qualified candidates like yourself must be turned down every year because of the lack of places in the entering class. Good luck with your future plans."

"I knew it!" Julia moaned. "Oh, wow, I wonder if the other letters will say the same thing. I *knew* I wasn't good enough to get in! I told you!"

"You are good, Julia," I said. "They just don't have room for everyone good, the way it said."

"If I was really special, they would," Julia argued. "See, the thing is I'm just not really special enough."

At supper, Mom and Dad tried to make Julia feel better. I could tell they were very disappointed themselves.

"Now, just wait till the other letters come before you let yourself feel too bad," Mom said.

"They're all going to say the same thing, wait and see," Julia said.

"I doubt it," said Dad. He lit another cigarette. He smokes too much, and when he is worried he smokes more. I wish they hadn't told us so much about cigarettes and cancer in school. I just hate to watch Dad smoke, because I know what may be happening to him.

"Wait and see," said Mom. "Wait and see, Julia. Don't give up yet."

That night was going to be my second time at the Estys. It turned out they liked me! And I think Jenny likes me, too. I read in a baby book they have that babies don't really smile until they're about six weeks old, but I think that's wrong. I am almost positive Jenny smiled at me the first night, and she is only four weeks old. I think she is probably very advanced for her age.

When Mrs. Esty first held her out to me, I was scared. I didn't know how to get her comfortable in my arms, and I was afraid I would drop her, with her mother watching! Then when I got her settled in my arms, Mrs. Esty told me to put her down in her crib. It's hard to do that the first time—you almost have to flip the baby over, and it feels like you're going to drop her. I was so awkward. But Mrs. Esty showed me how to put one hand under her stomach and one hand on her back, and turn her. The very first time I put her down, she didn't even cry. She just lay there quietly, as though she liked it.

Jenny has blue eyes, and a little bit of blond hair, and these tiny little hands and feet. If I put my finger inside her hand, she curls it right up around me. I have changed about six of her diapers by now, including some really messy yellow ones. It's sort of disgusting, but you clean it off fast with cotton and oil and shake on some cool powder and fold on a clean diaper, and wrap her up again in her little soft blanket and lay her back down in her bed, and she goes right to sleep. She's such a good baby.

I think the Estys will keep on wanting me for a baby-sitter. I hope so. I love their house. They have wonderful books and magazines. Last time, I read one of Mr. Esty's articles, about growing up on an Ohio farm. It was good. I told him I liked it, and he was really pleased. He cared about my opinion.

Yesterday after school I went to Chris's mother and asked her to make a bracelet for Julia for my graduation present. I told her just how I wanted it, so it will really be my design. It's going to be silver, about half an inch wide, very thick and very plain. I want Julia to have something like that, elegant and expensive. She is such a super person. It makes me happy to be planning the bracelet for her. It's going to cost a lot, maybe as much as thirty dollars. I told Mrs. Rosen I didn't want her to give me a special rate or anything. But she's going to let me pay for it slowly, a couple of dollars at a time. Now that I'm earning money from baby-sitting, I can afford it.

All of a sudden, I'm beginning to feel different. Ordering Julia's bracelet, explaining just how I want it, being able to pay for it with my own money. It feels grown up. I like it.

Fourteen

Talking to adults is funny. Some people treat you like a baby, and other people tell you what to do as though they owned you. A lot of people just don't seem to know how to talk with kids. I can't believe it when people actually say, "Oh, how you've grown!" Do they think this is some kind of brilliant remark? Karen says that someday she intends to answer back, "Maybe it's just that you've shrunk."

Of course, people always ask me if I am going to be as smart as my sister. How could anyone not understand that that is a mean question? I'm used to it, though, because teachers have asked me that since first grade. "Oh, I know your sister Julia. A lovely girl. Are you going to be smart like her?"

The Estys don't even know Julia, but that's not the reason I like to talk with them. The thing is, they really seem to like *me*. The last time I went there to baby-sit, they were finishing their dinner.

"You came just in time," Mrs. Esty said. "We cut

our piece of cheesecake into three slices so you could have one with us and then we ate ours up. We've been sitting here staring at your slice. You just about lost it!"

The cheesecake was delicious. But what I like about the Estys is, they wouldn't think it was strange or unusually kind to share their dessert with me. They just wanted to.

They were going to a party in Camden Woods. Mrs. Esty wrote down the phone number and told me to be sure to call if I had any questions at all.

"Jenny fussed a lot today," she said. "But I don't think you'll have trouble with her. She was so tired, she went to sleep the minute I put her down."

"There's a new book of short stories in my study that you might like to read, Cathy," Mr. Esty said. "I'm supposed to review it this week. It's by Nadine Gordimer. It has a red cover, and I think I put it on the floor about three piles to the left of the desk. Take a look if you want."

I love it that Mr. Esty suggests things to read, even though I feel very shy about giving my opinion afterward. Sometimes the books even have sexy parts in them. But they aren't stupid books—they're literature, like the books we read in English, only more for adults. I love to listen to the Estys talk about books. I guess that's what they want us to do in school, but in school your ideas always get mixed up with things like "characterization," and "mood," and "new vocabulary." With the Estys, you talk about opinions and feelings. Not just the author's, but theirs and mine, too.

Mrs. Esty went to Jenny's room for a last look, and Mr. Esty showed me where to find more soda if I drank up what was in the refrigerator.

"We'll probably stay till one, that is if you don't mind being up so late," he said.

"Oh, no, I really don't," I said. Time passes very fast at the Estys'. I'm usually surprised when they come back because I've been so busy reading or taking care of Jenny.

After they left, I went in to look at her. She has the prettiest room, white with blue-and-white curtains and a blue rug. She has a straw basket for car trips and a white crib to sleep in. There's a table to change her on and a rocking chair to rock her in. She already has books on her book shelf! Mrs. Esty says she couldn't wait to buy her some. And Mrs. Esty's own copy of *Peter Rabbit* and her whole set of *Little House* books are there, waiting for Jenny to grow up and read them. By the time Jenny's ready to read, I should know how to help her, because of my project with Mrs. Pflaum. I already know a lot about children's books. I've spent four afternoons in the library reading. There are some awfully good books for kids these days.

Jenny was asleep, lying on her stomach with one hand curled up near her head. She's so beautiful! It is just amazing to look at a little baby like her and realize that she is a *person* who will grow up and ride a bike and read books and maybe be a writer or a psychologist and have children of her own. Now that I have met Jenny, I think a lot about how people have children and those children have children, and how it goes on and on in waves. People being born, and growing up, and having babies, and dying. Dying of old age, or dying too young like George. I wish Jenny never had to die.

I found the book Mr. Esty told me about, and got an apple and took off my shoes and lay down on the Estys' couch. I love to be in their house by myself—by myself with Jenny, that is. I can almost imagine how it feels to be them, sitting in their own room reading a book with their own little baby sleeping softly nearby. It's so interesting to learn how other people live.

The phone rang. It was Karen.

"How're you doing?" she asked. "Listen, do you have to sit tomorrow?"

"They didn't say anything about it."

"Well, I just saw an ad for 'Miss America.' It's tomorrow night," Karen said. "Why don't you come and sleep over, and maybe Amy can, too."

"Oh, great," I said. "I'd love it. Maybe this year Bert Parks will drop dead on stage."

"Maybe this year Miss America will be six feet tall," Karen said.

Just then Jenny began to cry.

"I have to go," I said. "The baby's crying. See you tomorrow."

By the time I got to her room, Jenny was crying harder. I patted her back and talked to her—"It's OK, Jenny, go to sleep, honey,"—but she didn't stop. After a while I picked her up.

She was awfully hot. Of course, she was using a lot of energy, crying. It didn't sound like her usual cry, that starts low and rises and drops down again. This cry was a steady, high scream. Her face was red and puckered and her hands curled in tight little fists.

"What's the matter, Jenny?" I asked. I took her out to the kitchen for a bottle. Mrs. Esty breast-feeds her, but she has bottles between times. I had to hold onto her very tightly. She pushed against me so hard I thought she would bounce right out of my arms. I took the bottle from the fridge and warmed it under the hot water faucet and shook some on my wrist to test it, and the whole time this bundle of Jenny was pushing and screaming. She never stopped.

"Hey, Jenny," I said. "Don't cry anymore. Here's your nice bottle."

I sat down on a kitchen chair and put the bottle to her mouth. She screamed louder.

"Look, Jenny, it's your nice bottle. Take a little drink."

But Jenny wouldn't stop screaming. I put the bottle down, and I began to walk around the kitchen, rocking her softly in my arms. I felt her head again—it was still awfully hot.

I was getting worried. What if she kept on screaming, and I couldn't make her stop? What if she was sick? What if she wasn't sick, and I called the Estys at their party and told them she was?

"Come on, Jenny," I said. "Come on, honey. It's OK."

I carried her to the living room. Under the bright light her face looked almost purple. She was screaming without even stopping between screams. I laid her on my lap and felt her diapers, but they weren't wet. Under her little knit shirt her back was burning.

"Poor little Jenny," I said.

I walked around the living room for about ten minutes while Jenny kept screaming. I would have called Mom to ask what I should do, but she and Dad had gone to the movies. They wouldn't be home for an hour, at least. Julia was out somewhere with Nathan. I wanted to call the Estys, but I was afraid of worrying them for nothing. I decided to see if I could get help from their baby book. Jenny never stopped screaming while I went into their bedroom to find it.

It was hard to look something up with Jenny in my arms. I managed to turn to the S's, but there wasn't anything under *screaming*. In the C's I found *crying*. It said, "Sometimes a baby will cry very hard for minutes at a time for no apparent reason. If you find no obvious sources of discomfort, just walking with the baby may relieve the crying. If it persists, check the baby's temperature. A high temperature may be a sign of illness and the doctor should be called."

Jenny screamed while I read. I had done just what the book said, but walking around wasn't helping. She probably did have a temperature. I felt her head again and it was terribly hot. You have to use a rectal thermometer to take a baby's temperature. I had seen Mrs. Esty do it, but I was afraid to with Jenny kicking and screaming so hard. I opened up her blanket and lifted her shirt to feel her stomach. It was burning!

"Poor little thing," I told her.

I wrapped her up again and went right to the phone

to call the Estys. I had to, even if I would feel silly later. What would they think of me if Jenny was sick and I didn't tell them? It was hard to dial with the baby in my arms. She kept tightening up her legs and then pushing them out, stiff, and waving her little fists around her face. I was so relieved when I had dialed. But all I got at the house where the party was, was a busy signal.

I waited a minute and tried again. Still busy. So I decided that I ought to call the doctor myself. I looked up her name in their special phone book. Then I put Jenny on my lap with my hand on her back and dialed with the other hand. They answered! I could hardly hear, though, because of the screams.

"I'm calling about a baby, Jenny Esty," I said. "I'm her sitter. She seems to have a very high fever and she's screaming and I can't get her to stop."

"This is Dr. Elicoff's answering service," the voice said. "The doctor is out. Please leave your number and the doctor will get back to you very soon."

"How soon will it be?" I asked. I wished that Jenny would just stop screaming for a minute so I could hear better.

"I can't say exactly, miss," the voice said. "Please leave your message and the doctor will get it within an hour."

"Do you think it might be sooner?" I asked. I was beginning to be really scared. Jenny was gasping for breath between her screams.

"It will probably be within fifteen minutes," the voice said. "But I can't promise. Please leave your name and phone number, and Dr. Elicoff will call as soon as I can get hold of her."

I got up the nerve to say, "It's very important. I think the baby is awfully sick." Then I told the name and the number. The voice said, "Thank you," and there was a click. I was by myself again.

I tried the Estys' party another time, but the line was still busy. Can you imagine talking so long on the phone when the parents of a baby that might get sick were at your house? I think that was very thoughtless. If the Estys knew what was happening, they would have come right home. Since they didn't know, I had to do what I could by myself.

I looked up *fever* in the baby book. It said that one way to bring down a sudden high temperature was to cool off the baby with rubbing alcohol or water. I filled a cup with water and carried Jenny to the living room. Her screams were weaker now. I sat down on the couch with the cup on the coffee table and Jenny on her back on my lap. I unwrapped her blanket and unfastened her diapers and pulled one of her hot little arms out of her shirt sleeves. I poured water into my hand and rubbed it on Jenny's arm, the way the baby book said. She howled. The water must have felt awfully cold. I put that arm back in her shirt and took out the other one. Then I lifted the shirt up and put water on her stomach and turned her over and did her back. She seemed to calm down a little bit.

"You're going to feel better in a minute," I told her. "You're going to be OK." I thought she felt cooler already. I kept patting the water onto her body. She was so tiny! I wondered how it would feel to be so small and so hot. Her legs seemed to relax and I thought her screams were slowing down.

I wrapped the blanket loosely around her. Without her clothes she was such a small bundle—her little behind was just nothing without her diaper. I thought I should surely be able to reach the Estys, but when I tried their number was still busy. I tried our house. Mom answered!

I told her what had happened.

"How is she now?" Mom asked.

"Lying in my arms, much quieter. She's cooler. Oh, Mom, it was so scary!"

"You did just the right thing, Catherine," Mom said. "I'm proud of you."

"Do you think I should call the Estys anyway?"

Mom said they would surely want to know. "I'll be right here if you need help. But I think you'll be fine."

Finally, ten minutes later, I got the house where the party was. I just hated to scare Mrs. Esty by asking for her. When she came to the phone, sort of breathless, the first thing I said was, "Jenny is fine." And she was. She was sleeping on my lap.

The Estys came right home. Mrs. Esty ran in and took Jenny from me and hugged her.

Then they wanted to know all the details.

"Oh, Cathy," Mrs. Esty said, "to think of us sitting at that party and not knowing. It wasn't even a very interesting party! Oh, how could we have stayed so long!"

The phone rang. It was the doctor. I heard Mrs. Esty say that the baby-sitter had managed beautifully.

She threw me a kiss as I went out the door with Mr. Esty.

He didn't say much on the way home. But after he paid me, he put his hand on my arm and said, "Cathy, you know we're indebted to you. Thank you. Mary and I are very happy to have you helping with Jenny."

Mom made me a toasted cheese sandwich. She and Dad sat in the kitchen with me while I ate. All of a sudden I realized how tired I was.

"I'm exhausted!" I said.

"You've worked hard," Dad said.

I kissed them goodnight and went upstairs and got undressed, and fell into bed without even brushing my teeth.

Fifteen

Karen has her own TV, and her bedroom is neat for watching. There are two wicker chairs with yellow cushions and a beige rug about three inches thick to sit on, and big floor pillows covered with pink and orange cloth her mother bought in Mexico.

Karen and Amy were already upstairs when I came. That meant I had to talk to Karen's mother when she came to the door. Karen's mother always makes me feel uncomfortable. I know she means to be friendly, but it seems as though she has to work at it. I think she wants to talk to me on my level, but she doesn't know where my level is.

"That's a nifty shirt, Cathy," she said. "Very slimming."

I wondered how fat I must usually look to her.

"Thanks," I said.

She said, "The girls are upstairs, so I suppose you'll

want to go right on up and not stay down here talking to us two old bags." She laughed and looked toward the living room, where Mrs. Adams, her neighbor, was sitting on the couch in bright green pants and a bright pink top, smoking a cigarette.

"OK," I said.

Karen's mother sort of traps you. I don't think she and Mrs. Adams are old bags, but I didn't exactly know how to say so. I would feel dumb saying, "You are not an old bag, Mrs. Curtis." It's so hard to say what I mean to her that I usually don't say much at all. I went on up the stairs, and I heard Karen's mother laughing in the living room.

I knocked on Karen's door and went right in.

"Am I on time?"

"You made it, it's only quarter of," Karen said.

"Hey, Cathy," Amy said. "How was sitting?"

"Scary," I said. "Jenny got this high fever all of a sudden, and I couldn't get hold of the doctor and Mom was out and the phone at the Estys' party was busy."

"What did you do?" Karen asked. "I wouldn't know what to do. I'd probably just get hysterical."

I told them about it. It was hard to remember how scared I'd been at the time. It was over so fast.

"Babies get hot awfully suddenly," Amy said. She knows because of her sisters. She never goes out to baby-sit because she has to do it all the time at home. Her mother and father go out a lot and she has to take care of the little kids. Her parents don't pay her. I don't think that's fair.

Karen said, "I don't know how people have the nerve to have babies at all, so many things can go wrong with them."

"And you have to watch them every minute," said Amy. "That's why I'm not going to have any."

"Oh, Amy, how can you say that now?" Karen said. "Wait till you grow up and get married. You'll want to have a baby just like everyone else."

"I'm not going to *be* like everyone else," Amy said.

I bet she won't, either. Maybe she'll play her flute with orchestras all over the world. It would be fun to go to her concerts.

"Hey, it's time," Karen said. She turned the set on and after a minute music blared out, and you could see all the contestants doing some kind of dance. Every single one of them was smiling.

Bert Parks came on. We cheered.

"There he is," I said. "Mr. Asinine."

The funniest thing about Bert Parks is that he really believes "Miss America" is an important event. "And now the moment these beautiful and talented young ladies have worked for with such dedication is almost here. . . " he said.

He began to introduce the candidates. Those poor girls always have names that make you laugh. This year Miss Nevada was Donna Mae Cusp. Miss Tennessee was Linda Grubber. But the name that really broke us up was Mary Alice Birdwhistle, Miss Louisiana. Even Bert Parks had trouble with that one.

"I'm sure all the fellows whistle at *you*," he said, "ha, ha."

"Mary Alice Birdwhistle!" Karen shouted. "Can you imagine, 'Here she comes, Mary Alice Birdwhistle, my ideal.' "

Amy said, "I hope she wins, so they have to suffer with her name for a whole year."

We decided to root for her, but you could just tell she wouldn't win. We thought Miss New Hampshire might. She had an enormous bosom.

"It's practically indecent," Karen said.

Amy said, "That's what people are supposed to like, a big bust, like in *Playboy* pictures. I wonder if it's really true, though. My cousin got married to this man who likes her a lot, and she's practically flat-chested."

I said, "I certainly would not marry anyone who just cared about the size of my bust."

"Anyway," Karen said, "my mother says how you look isn't so important, it's what you make of it."

I didn't say this, but I can't stand the idea of trying to *make* something of your looks all the time. No matter how hard I worked, I would never look like the women in Karen's mother's magazine. I like to look good, but I don't want to make it my lifework. I wonder how important it really is.

"People always say beauty is only skin deep," Amy said, "but if your skin is broken out or your nose is enormous or you're really fat, I don't see how that would be much comfort."

"I know it," I said. "They say looks aren't important, and then they keep on having beauty pageants."

Bert Parks was back. "These lovely ladies have now reached the semifinal stage of their gallant journey and started the climb toward the summit: the Miss America title!"

"Oh, no," Amy moaned. "How can anyone be so dumb? How old do you suppose Bert Parks is?"

"Old enough to be my great-grandfather," Karen said fast. We laughed.

It was evening gown time. The ten finalists waltzed across the stage in horrible dresses with ruffles.

"My, they're lovely," Bert Parks said. "You know, there's something about a girl in an evening dress. . . ."

"That makes you want to throw up," Karen finished.

I said, "Karen, where do you suppose you'll be next year for 'Miss America'?"

"Not here, anyway," Karen said.

"I suppose you'll have a lot of new friends at boarding school," said Amy.

"Sure," Karen said. "So will you two have lots of new friends in high school."

That's true. I hadn't thought of that so much. "Still, we'll miss you," I said.

"I'll come home for holidays," Karen said.

"It won't be the same," Amy said. "Nothing ever is."

Karen said, "Yeah. I feel kind of scared about going away."

"Oh, Karen," I burst out. "I thought you *wanted* to go away."

"Well, I do," she said. "But then sometimes I wonder if my mother wants it more. In some ways, I wish I was staying here."

It's funny. Deciding what to do is hard for everybody. Being rich like Karen doesn't seem to make it easier. You can afford more things, but that doesn't help you choose which to do.

It was talent show time.

Amy said, "Look. Every single one of them is going to be an acrobatic dancer."

"Some of them always sing," I said.

"They always sing a song called 'Shoo-Fly Pie and Apple-Pan-Dowdy,' " Karen said. But she was wrong. Miss Wyoming sang "The Lord's Prayer."

"That's what they sang at George Waldman's funeral," Amy said. "How could she want to sing it for a beauty pageant?"

All of a sudden we remembered about George Waldman. It's strange how it comes and goes. For a couple of days after he died, that's all I thought about. Everybody talked about it in school. People went to the funeral. Our bus seemed different. Our human relations class got more serious. But then, I noticed that I forgot about it sometimes. Now it's like something bad that suddenly comes into my mind, and then after a while it goes away, until it suddenly comes back again.

"I heard his father is still here," Amy said. "Maybe this will bring his parents together again."

"They must be glad to have each other to talk to," said Karen.

I hoped so. It's hard for me to talk when I'm worried, but I feel better when I can. I know that now, because of the suspension. When I could finally talk to my family, they really helped.

The pageant announcer was a lady who had once been Miss America herself. "I can tell you," she said, as though she was sharing a wonderful secret, "that for the girls backstage, the excitement and anxiety are reaching fever pitch."

It was the bathing suit competition.

"I would die," I said, "before I would stand up in front of anybody in my own bathing suit, much less one of those silver corsets, and have people judge the size of my behind."

"I suppose some of them do it for the scholarship money," Amy said.

I thought about Julia. I suppose nobody would choose Julia for Miss America, but if anyone deserves a scholarship, it's her. I wished she would hear from Yale and Barnard soon.

Bert Parks introduced the five finalists. Mary Alice Birdwhistle was not one of them. Miss New Hampshire was. All the other candidates squealed and clapped for the finalists. I wondered how they really felt.

"And now," Bert Parks said, "to give our audience a chance to evaluate the candidates' ability to speak with poise and grace, I'm going to talk briefly with each one."

He asked Miss New Hampshire how many people were in her family. She said five. Fast thinking. Everybody clapped. Then he asked her the deep one.

"Many people believe that time has the power to soothe away our troubles. Do you?"

Then Miss New Hampshire said this funny thing. She was trying to think fast and sound smart, and you could tell she was scared to death even though she kept smiling. She said, "Oh, yes, I always say, 'Time wounds all heals.'"

"Hey, did you hear that?" Karen shouted. "She said, 'wounds all heels'!"

"Wounds all heels!" we yelled. "Wounds all heels!"

Bert Parks looked puzzled. He lowered the microphone and mumbled something to Miss New Hampshire. "I think maybe you've got that a little backward," he said into the mike, patting Miss New Hampshire's shoulder "Want to try it again?"

Miss New Hampshire smiled broadly. "Oh, sure," she said. "What I meant to say was, 'Time wounds all heals.' That is, if we just wait long enough, everything will be OK."

Bert Parks gave up. "Well, thank you very much, let's give her a big hand, ladies and gentlemen—Miss New Hampshire!"

In the end, Miss New Hampshire did not win. Neither did Miss Delaware, who we thought would. Miss Missouri was second runner-up. Miss Idaho and Miss Pennsylvania were left, hugging each other and sobbing and waiting to find out which one would be Miss America. There were drum rolls. The contestants shrieked and the audience yelled and Bert Parks shouted, "Ladies and gentlemen, the first runner-up, Miss *Idaho*!" That meant Miss Idaho lost, and Miss Pennsylvania was Miss America. So she and Miss Idaho screamed and cried. Then Miss Pennsylvania kissed the old Miss America, and kissed Bert Parks, and Bert Parks put a crown on her head, and someone gave her flowers, and there she was, Miss America, sobbing her heart out on the runway. And there I was, singing that dopey song along with Bert Parks under my breath.

"I hate myself!" said Amy. "I'm crying. How can I be so dumb?"

In fact, we were all crying. There was not a dry eye in Karen's room.

"We're crazy!" I said. "How can we cry for Miss America when so many things are really sad?"

"Never mind," Karen said. "Remember, 'time wounds all heels'!"

We sat there laughing and crying and feeling like dopes. It was fun. I wouldn't miss "Miss America" for anything.

Sixteen

I worked in the yearbook office after school every day the next week. At first, I was really shy. It didn't seem as though I belonged there because I was only an eighth-grader. I couldn't stand for anyone to think I was trying to sneak in because of my sister.

But Julia said it wasn't like that at all. "We really need all the help we can get," she said. "Everybody will be glad to have you. *I'm* glad."

I loved the office. Mr. Altman, the advisor, was as nice as Julia said. The first day I came, he made a big fuss over me.

"Another one!" he said. "One Myers is special enough. With two of them, we should be able to beat any deadline they can set."

But it wasn't easy. There were all these long galley proofs of seniors' names that had to be checked for exact spelling on top of all the other printed stuff. I worked with another girl, a tenth-grader named Alice Hendricks. I would read her the words on the typed copy they sent to the printer, and she would check them against what actually got printed. That's called proof-reading. To change some mistake, Alice would make a sign in the margin of the galley proof. The sign told the printer what to do, like capitalize a letter or close up an empty space or fix a word that was spelled wrong.

"How do you ever learn all the symbols?" I asked Alice.

"It's not hard," she said. "You do them a few times and you learn them. The first time, I looked up each sign in a proofreader's book."

Finally, all the pages were checked. I never realized before how many mistakes you could have in any one book. You could spell things wrong or mix up page numbers or put wrong captions under pictures. Now that I know all this, I think it is a miracle so many books come out perfect. In a yearbook, spelling people's names wrong is the worst mistake that could possibly happen. So we checked each name at least two different times.

On the Friday afternoon when everything was ready for the printer, Mr. Altman came in with sandwiches and soda from The Break. "OK, you workers," he said, "time out for a celebration."

It was really nice in that office. I was proud to be related to Julia. Everyone asked her questions, and she knew almost all the answers.

"Going to go out for the yearbook next year?" Alice asked me.

"Oh, I don't know," I said. "I didn't think freshmen usually did that."

"No reason why not," she said. "Especially you. You've got a good head start. We all know how hard you can work. Everyone who's here next year would like to have you."

I would love to work on the yearbook next year. Julia didn't even start till she was in tenth grade. If I begin in ninth grade, who knows, I might get to be one of the editors when I'm a senior. It's not that I want to do the same things Julia did. It's just that now I've worked on the yearbook I know how interesting it is. I can't wait till the book is printed, and I can really see Nathan's pictures. Lots of kids in my school have ordered the yearbook. It'll be fun when it comes out.

Mr. Altman drove Julia and me home. It was six o'clock. Mr. Altman sang songs the whole way: "Cockles and Mussels," and "Tea for Two." It seems that's a sign that he's feeling especially good.

When we got out, he said, "Julia, I just want to say that it's the best school yearbook I've ever seen. And it's largely due to you. You should be very proud."

Julia said, "Nathan, too."

"What's Nathan going to do next year, anyway?" asked Mr. Altman.

"He's going to Camden Community," Julia said, "and take photography on the side."

I couldn't help thinking that Julia and Nathan would be separated if Julia got into Barnard or Yale. I wonder how much Julia would miss him? It must be strange to stop seeing someone you've seen every day for years.

Mr. Altman reached out and shook my hand. "Thank

you for your help, Cathy," he said. "Will we see you next year?"

"I hope so," I said.

"I hope so, too," he said. "So long, girls."

There were two strange cars in front of our house.

"I know," Julia said. "It's Mom's cleaning lady meeting."

It was. Mom called out to us when we went inside "Come and say hello," she said. We went in and got introduced. "Mrs. Johnson, Mrs. Green, Mrs. Moses, Mrs. Saltera, Mrs. Washington," Mom said. "These are my girls, Julia and Catherine."

They all smiled and said, "Oh, what big girls!" and things like that. All of them except Mrs. Saltera were black. I guess we never had black people in our house before. But Mom looked very comfortable. She and the others were talking and laughing a lot.

"Get yourselves a snack, will you?" Mom asked. "I know it's late, and we're just coming to the end of our meeting. We don't want to interrupt now."

Julia and I went out to the kitchen.

"Hey!" I said.

There was a letter for Julia on the table. From Yale. Julia opened the envelope and unfolded the letter. She held her face very stiff while she read it. Then she whispered, "Oh! Oh, Cathy, look!"

I read as far as, "The admissions office of Yale University is pleased to inform you of your acceptance, with full scholarship—"

"Julia!" I shouted. "Hey, go tell Mom!"

"Wait till she's finished, Cath," Julia said.

But I couldn't wait. I ran to the doorway. "Mom!" I said. "Listen to Julia's news!"

"What?" said Mom. "What is it, Julia?"

Julia said, "Mom, I got into Yale. With the scholarship."

All the women stopped talking. Mom got up and ran to hug Julia. "Oh, Julia!"

"Yale!" said Mrs. Moses. "Now isn't that something!"

I went to dial Dad's number so Julia could tell him. But his phone didn't answer. That meant he was on his way home. I ran outside to see him when he turned in the driveway.

Right then, I heard his car.

"Hey, Dad!" I called. "Dad! Hurry up!"

Dad stopped the car by the door and rolled down his window. "What's that?" he said, smiling.

"Come and hear Julia's news!"

Dad opened the door and jumped out. "Where is she?"

Then Julia ran out. "Dad," she said, "I made it! I got into Yale with a scholarship!"

Dad and Julia and I hugged and laughed in the front yard. If the neighbors saw us they must have thought we'd gone crazy. But that was one of the most exciting days our family ever had. Julia was going to Yale!

When we finally sat down to eat, Mom told us about her meeting. She and the other women had decided to put an ad in the paper and be a housecleaning cooperative. They would use our phone number, and Mom or Julia or I would take the calls when we were home and set up appointments for all the women. Everybody would ask for three dollars an hour, and none of them would work before nine or after six.

"It's like a union," Julia said.

"It is," said Mom. "It's also like a business, because we'll be managing the schedule and the payment. Working together, we can cover for each other if someone needs a day off or if anyone wants to work extra. We'll see. It's going to be complicated at first, and the phone will bother us for a while till we settle down. But I think it will work out just fine in the end. These are good women, you know," she said. "Good family women who care about each other. I'm lucky to have met them."

That's just like Mom. She would make friends wherever she goes. She's that kind of person.

You might think that was enough excitement for one night. But there was more. The next thing was that the phone rang. It was for me.

"Cathy, could you sit tomorrow night?" Mrs. Esty asked.

"Oh, sure," I said. Julia's bracelet was one-third paid for by now. Mrs. Rosen had almost finished it. I was eager to earn the rest of the money.

"And, Cathy," Mrs. Esty said. "I want to tell you now that we're going to ask you something when you come. So you can be thinking it over ahead of time. What we're wondering is, if you would consider coming to Maine with us, to our summer place, for a couple of weeks this summer and help us look after Jenny. I don't want you to say yes or no now. Think it over and talk about it with your parents, and we can talk more tomorrow when you come."

"I already know I'd love to!" I said.

"Well, I don't want you to decide too fast," said Mrs. Esty. "You know very well it's a lot of work, taking care of a baby. Of course, we'd want you to have some free time. There are other kids around that you could swim with. We'd be able to pay you twenty-five dollars a week besides your room and board. It's a beautiful place, and we'd love to have you there with us. So, think it over."

I never expected anything like that! Imagine, going to Maine with the Estys. I'll probably feel shy at first. But I like them so much. And I love little Jenny. And Maine! I've never been as far as Maine in my whole life.

"Guess what," I told Mom and Dad and Julia. "I'm going to go to Maine! That is, if you let me. Oh, wow! Maine!"

Then we had more hugs. My family was truly happy for me.

Later that night Mom called Aunt Rose to tell her about Julia's scholarship.

"Tell her Yale gave Julia the scholarship because she always stood up straight," I said.

"Catherine!" Mom scolded.

But she laughed, and so did Dad. Usually they hate

for me and Julia to talk like that. I could tell Mom was glad to be able to tell Aunt Rose about Julia. She told her about me going to Maine, too, right away.

Do you know what Aunt Rose said? Mom told me afterwards, like a private joke just between us.

"Rose said it was wonderful about Julia," Mom laughed. "But to tell you that they have terrible black flies in Maine."

"Oh, Mom," I said. "I can't wait to see them!"

Seventeen

Some people thought we ought to have a real graduation from eighth grade. But I was glad we weren't going to. I hate formal, stuffy programs with benedictions and class songs and citizenship awards. We had one of those in sixth grade. It was at noon on a hot June day and I was wearing tights. I nearly fainted, and when everyone stood up to sing "The Battle Hymn of the Republic," I had to keep on sitting down. It was embarrassing. I think people should just have big ceremonies for certain important things, like high-school graduation or weddings, and make other times be more like a party. We're going to have a big picnic with food we bring from home after our special eighth-grade assembly, the week after high-school graduation. That should be fun.

Before the assembly, the whole school is going to go outside and plant a tree for George Waldman. His mother's coming, and I think his father too. I don't see how they can bear it. Still, I think planting a tree is a good memorial. The tree will keep growing, and people will remember.

June always seems more like the real end of the year than December. A lot of end-of-the-year things were happening. I wrote up a long report on my project for Mrs. Inman. It's the most work I've ever done for a class in school. I wrote reviews of two books and one magazine article, and a summary of my talks with Mrs. Pflaum. Then I did a separate paper with Bobby Arvin's opinions about four different children's books I read with him. It took me a week to finish the project and I worked every afternoon and every night. I took it along when I went baby-sitting. Mrs. Esty was very interested. She knew some of the books because she used them with children at Eastern State.

When I put my report together, it was fifteen pages long! I was surprised. So was Mrs. Inman.

"Goodness, Cathy, you did some hard work on this," she said when I gave her my folder. It was red, with a title I had printed on white paper and pasted on: "Helping First Grade Children to Read." I liked handing in a project I felt so good about. Next year I am going to organize a group of people to help at Allen School. They can be high-school and junior-high kids. A good thing is that I'll keep in touch with Mrs. Inman that way. She's my best teacher so far.

Then the yearbook came out. Lots of kids in my school, especially the eighth-graders, got them. The big thing was to look for a picture of yourself in it and then to go around and get people to sign your book.

There was a good picture of me. I was sitting in the big chair at home reading. I didn't even know that Nathan took it. Chris made me sign it in his book. I wasn't sure what to write, so I just said, "Love to Chris from Cathy." I gave the book back to him and he read it and said, "Thanks, Cathy. That's nice."

I suppose everyone who works on a yearbook says, "This year's is special," but this one really was. I'm not just saying that because my sister edited it or because I helped out. The cover was very dramatic—black with white tree branches across it and the year in white letters. A big change inside was that the senior portraits, those formal studio pictures where the boys wear jackets and ties and the girls all wear a dumb velvet drape that belongs to the photographer, were reduced to tiny squares so they fitted on the inside of the front and back covers. Julia used the pages she saved that way for Nathan's big candid photographs of the seniors the way they really look, wearing jeans and working or eating lunch or talking.

Pictures of teachers and the administration and school custodians were mixed right in with pictures of kids. Bad things about Camden High were there: trash against the back of the building, the traffic jam on Clark Street after school, the main hall with nobody in it, long and dark as a prison. There were pictures of kids arguing and there was one of some kid breaking a branch off a tree. But most of the pictures showed people working, laughing, doing things. Anyone who saw the yearbook would have a good picture of Camden High. It made me want to go there.

At the bottom of each page there was a line of words that ran straight through the book. It was a kind of diary of the school year. My favorite page had pictures of kids talking with teachers. The words said:

What we know is just the start of knowing;
What we learned is how to keep on growing.

Julia stayed late at the yearbook office the day it came out. They were having a cheese and punch party in the office, and then they were going out to dinner together. They asked me, but I had promised Mom to come home on the early bus and answer the phone for the housecleaning group. In a way, I was glad for a reason not to go out with the yearbook staff. I had only done a little work, and I didn't really belong yet. Next year, I will.

There were a lot of phone calls for Mom. Some people just wanted information on rates, but other people called to make dates for a couple of weeks ahead. I think it's very good to set up the work that way. When people have to arrange for your days each time, they can't think they own you. Also, now Mom and her friends had set hours they would work, so they knew ahead of time when they'd be home. Unless they worked overtime. But they only did that if they got paid time-and-a-half the usual rate. They figured that other people get overtime, so why shouldn't house-workers? Being part of a group made Mom's work seem more dignified. I noticed that I didn't really mind talking about it anymore. I know Dad was glad that Mom had better pay and working conditions. And

Mom seemed to enjoy all the details and arrangements. She made about ten phone calls every morning before work. I think she likes managing things.

The next call was for me. "Oh, hi, Amy," I said. "I didn't expect to hear you. The phone's always ringing for Mom's group."

"Did anyone call Julia?" Amy asked.

"Not this afternoon."

"Did anybody say anything to you about the yearbook?"

"Just that they liked it. What do you mean?"

"I don't know if I should say." She sounded so ominous and mysterious that I couldn't stand it.

"What are you talking about, Amy?"

"Well, listen, Mom ran into Cindy Bergman's mother in the deli, and Mrs. Bergman said the yearbook was a disgrace."

"A *disgrace?*" I couldn't believe it.

"She said, 'They've ruined Cindy's beautiful studio portrait that we paid twenty dollars for.'"

"Didn't she see the candid shots?"

"I don't know, Cathy. I just thought I ought to warn you."

I said, "Thanks, Amy. See you tomorrow."

I wondered if this was the start of something awful. The phone rang again.

"Is Julia there?" a familiar voice said.

"No, she isn't," I said.

"Is this Cathy?" the voiced asked. Suddenly I recognized it. It was Karen's mother. I wondered if she was going to complain, too.

"Oh, hi, Mrs. Curtis," I said. "Julia will be home later."

"Well, I'll call back," Karen's mother said. "I really must talk to her. I want to tell her that I think her yearbook is marvelous. I'm really impressed. I've seen lots of professional work that isn't as polished as this."

"Thanks!" I said. "I'll tell Julia you called."

Was I glad she called just then. Otherwise I think I would have been too influenced by Mrs. Bergman's opinion. This way I realized that she was only one person, and just because she didn't like the yearbook, that didn't make it bad. When you do something creative and different you have to expect some people not to like it.

I was very impressed that Mrs. Curtis liked it. After all, she is a real magazine editor and she ought to know. I hoped she noticed that she was complimenting something from Camden High. Maybe this would make her change her opinion about it.

Of course, Mom and Dad loved the yearbook. They put my copy on the kitchen table and read every page together. When Julia came home, Mom went all through it again with her. Mom kept seeing pictures of kids she remembered from grade school.

"Benny Ferris! Remember how you used to call him Benny Ferris Wheel? And look at Cheryl Nyland, all grown up. My, what a pretty girl she turned out to be."

It must be strange to be a parent and see time pass and your kids grow up. You must always be surprised. Maybe *that's* why people say, "How you've grown!"—

because they're surprised. I think I can understand that. I'm surprised at Jenny every time I see her. It's funny to think that some day she'll be a kid my age. I'll probably tell her, "Oh, Jenny, how you've grown!"

Eighteen

Julia's graduation dress was beautiful. It was light blue cotton with little white flowers. Long sleeves, a ruffle around the hem, and a wide sash. Of course it would be all covered up by her white gown, but she would wear it to the party afterward.

I sat on her bed and watched her brush her hair. My silver bracelet slipped up and down her arm. It looked elegant, just the way I had hoped. Julia had cried and hugged me when I gave it to her.

"Oh, Cath!" she said. "How did you know? I always wished for something as beautiful as this. But I never expected to have it. Thank you! I'll think of you whenever I wear it."

It was certainly worth my thirty dollars to please Julia that much. It was just what I wanted.

"I'm so nervous!" Julia said now.

"You shouldn't be," I told her. "You look beautiful, and your speech is so good."

She had practiced it on Mom and Dad and me last night. It *was* good—not the usual stuff about how this generation will carry on the great traditions, etcetera. Julia's speech was about planning. Why she was going to be a city planner and why people should plan ahead for their lives and not just let fate overtake them.

"Julia!" Mom called up the stairs. "It's time! Dad's all ready to take you. For goodness' sake, this is one time you don't want to be late."

"I'm coming, Mom," Julia shouted back. "Oh, Cath," she said to me, "I feel so funny, you know? Like it's the end of the world. I have to wait all summer to find out what college will be like. And sometimes I feel so sad to think about leaving you, and Mom and Dad." She sat down on the bed next to me. "I'm going to miss you, Cath, you know?"

"Oh, Julia!" I said, hugging her. "I'm going to miss *you.*"

I was actually crying, and when I tried to smile at Julia, I saw that she was crying too. This made us both cry harder. At the same time, we were laughing at ourselves. Laughing and crying, both—it's true, you can do it.

Mom came upstairs and found us like that.

"Oh, girls," she said. "Come on, now. You don't want to cry at a happy time like this." She looked as though she might break into tears herself.

"Stand up and let me see you, Julia," she said.

So Julia stood up and wiped her eyes and gave her hair another brush. "There," she said. "How do I look?"

Mom did have tears in her eyes. But she was smiling, too. "You look beautiful," she said. "Just beautiful. Now come down and show your father, quickly. You barely have time to make it to school by seven-thirty."

Julia laughed. "I have never in my whole life known them to set a sensible time to get to school for a program. Even in grade school. They always threatened you about what would happen if you didn't come an hour early. And then when you got there you just had to sit around and wait. By concert time kids were nervous and excited. Somebody always threw up."

"Never mind," Mom said. "You of all people are going to be on time tonight."

"Clara!" Dad shouted up. "Is she coming? She's going to be late!"

Julia ran out. "I'm coming, Dad," she called.

I ran after her. "See you, Julia. You'll be wonderful. Look for me."

Julia turned. "So long, Cath," she smiled. She looked different already.

Mom started down the stairs, then turned back. "Catherine. Now get right into the shower and get dressed fast. I intend for us to leave this house promptly at eight. It's going to be hard to find a parking place at school, and we can't be late. This night of all nights."

The phone rang and Dad answered. "It's for you, Julia. Aunt Rose."

Julia ran to the phone.

Mom yelled, "Don't talk long! Tell Rose you have to go!"

It was nice of Aunt Rose to call, but she certainly had bad timing. She wasn't going to the graduation. There weren't enough seats for all of people's relatives. Seniors only got tickets for their parents, brothers and sisters, and grandparents. If you didn't have grandparents, you still didn't get extra tickets. Aunt Rose felt bad about that and I could understand why. But in private I was glad to be going to Julia's graduation with just my mom and dad.

I took a shower and put on my new dress. It was a long white Mexican dress with blue embroidery around the square neck. I loved it. Mom had wanted me to get it even though it was pretty expensive. "I want you to look especially nice for your sister's graduation," she said, "but that's not the only reason. You need something pretty to wear when you go out, now that you're growing up."

I was going to go to two parties. One was at Chris's and one at Karen's. They would be next week. I was looking forward to them. I had never gone to a real party with invitations and everything before.

I looked at myself in the mirror. I wondered if I looked like a ninth-grader. I thought I probably did. I was even getting taller, it looked like.

For once my hair went the way I wanted it to. But my eyes were sort of washed out from crying. I ran into Julia's room and found her eyebrow pencil and mascara and brought them back. It was easy to make my eyebrows darker with the pencil, but the mascara was different. There doesn't seem to be such a thing as a little bit of mascara. Either you don't use any or you get great big blobs all over your eyelashes. I had blobs. I blinked, and they smudged over my face. I looked stupid.

"Cathy!" Mom called. "Dad's back. We'll leave in five minutes. Are you ready?"

"Almost," I yelled down. I ran into the bathroom and tried to wash the mascara off my face. Why did I have to go and fool with it at a time like this? It wouldn't come off even though I scrubbed with soap. The soap stung my eyes. I was going to be the laughing-stock of the whole graduation! Finally, I thought of cold cream. I put some on my face and eyelashes and wiped it off with toilet paper. Thank goodness, the mascara came off.

"Catherine!"

"I'm coming," I called. I ran down the steps.

Dad was standing in the hall looking impatient. But he smiled when he saw me. "You certainly look pretty, Catherine," he said. "All set, now?"

Mom hugged me. "You look lovely," she said. "We'll be the best-looking family at graduation, if I say so myself."

Dad had on his gray suit and a blue tie. Mom was wearing a new navy blue dress with white beads and earrings. We did look nice. It was funny to be so dressed up on a Wednesday night.

And it was strange to sit alone in the back seat of the car with Mom and Dad up front. Now we'd be a family of just three people most of the time. I was going to miss Julia terribly. But in a way, it might be fun to be an only child.

It seemed unreal, like in a movie, to drive along the bus route streets in the evening. We passed other dressed-up people getting into cars. The sun was setting and there was gold light on the trees and grass. Everything seemed ordinary and beautiful at the same time.

We drove past George Waldman's house. I wondered if his mother knew it was graduation night. Just think, she will never get to watch George grow up and graduate. It seems so awful that he died before he had the chance to get older. This year—the year his life stopped—seems like just the beginning of mine. Everything is so new—going to high school, going to Maine. . . .

I wonder how my life will turn out. It's going to be interesting to see.

People Called Me A Nut

"My book is not the kind that tells 'How Tomboy Mindy discovered that growing up gracefully can be as fun as playing baseball.'

"I have often thought how relaxing it would be to be invisible. But when I took over Richard's paper route they said 'girls can't deliver papers.' And when I wanted to take tennis instead of slimnastics, they said 'girls like to do graceful feminine things.' So I had to speak out. I only wanted things to be fair.

"My book is for anyone who might want to read about the life and thoughts of a person like me. If some boy wants to read this, go ahead. Maybe you will learn something."

The Real Me
by Betty Miles

An AVON CAMELOT BOOK
Code: 65292-7 • $2.25

You can't tell a friend by her looks—
or a book by its cover!

MAUDIE AND ME
and the
DIRTY BOOK

✱ ✱ ✱

By
BETTY MILES

author of *The Trouble With Thirteen*

*"To look at me, you'd probably think I was pretty
ordinary—except for my feet, which are size 9½M.
You wouldn't expect me to get into trouble at school,
or wreck little children's minds with dirty books."*

For Kate Harris, getting used to life in middle school
means figuring out where to sit in the cafeteria, and
avoiding kids like Maudie Schmidt. But then Kate
and Maudie are thrown together in a school reading
project, and a book that Kate reads to some first
graders sparks an angry controversy. Kate finds
herself in the middle as the whole town takes sides
and demands for censorship grow. And in the midst
of the uproar, Kate discovers that Maudie is not only
her staunchest ally, but a true friend.

AN AVON CAMELOT • 64071-6 • $2.25